Emma

C000228735

PETER GUNNING

BLACKWATER PRESS

First published in 1997
by Blackwater Press,
Unit 7/8, Broomhill Business Park,
Tallaght,
Dublin 24

Printed at the press of the publishers.

Managing Editor: Deirdre Whelan
Editor: Zoë O'Connor
Cover Design: Philip Ryan
Cover Illustration: Tom Roche
ISBN: 0 86121 919 8
British Library Cataloguing-in-Publication Data.
A catalogue record for this book is available from the British Library.
Gunning, Peter. Kick the Can.

CONTENTS

For Finbarr and Sinéad
also
Thanks, Dad!

Note on the Author
Peter Gunning was born in London in 1959
and grew up in Birmingham and Cork.
He is the author of the comic novel *Stanley* and
the best-selling teenage thriller, *Reaching the Heights,*
both of which are published by Blackwater Press.
Peter is a teacher and lives in Midleton, Co Cork.

Chapter 1

Nightwork

"Would ye stop kicking that bloody can! It's half past eight in the morning! There are people up here trying to get some sleep!"

"Sorry, Tanker!" came the half-apology as the game came to a temporary end and Tanker scrambled back into his bed. Less than a minute later the familiar rat-a-tat-tat started up again, accompanied by the equally familiar running commentary from Aidan Dunne.

"And Bomber has it now as he races past Poncho, he looks up and sees Spudser perfectly placed in front of goal... "

Tanker made his way over to the window and looked down to where the game was taking place. It was the FA Cup Final between Liverpool and Manchester United in the thirty square metre car park of Terence MacSwiney Mansions. According to nine-year-old Dunnzer, who as well as commentating for the benefit of the entire estate was also keeping goal for United, the score was twenty seven all.

"And as we come up to half-time, Liverpool seem to be losing pace as United keep pressing forward for goal number twenty eight... "

"You can't say that, Dunnzer!" complained the Liverpool skipper six-year-old Froggie, otherwise known as Fergus Fahy.

"Get lost, Froggie! I can say what I like! I'm up here in the commentary box!"

Dunnzer ignored the whining of Froggie and became ecstatic as Bomber, otherwise known as Bernard Daly, scored that all-important goal number twenty eight.

The game was unusual in many respects, not the least of

which was the fact that it was being played with a much-battered coke can. Tanker's head was bursting from the constant grating sound of aluminium on tarmac. He opened the window and interrupted the game again.

"Hey, Dunnzer!" he shouted. Dunnzer took his fist out of his mouth and looked up to the fourth floor.

"Sorry, Tanker! We're finished now. We'll go away!"

"That's what you said the last twenty times! Here, catch this!"

Tanker threw down his plastic football. It bounced with a resounding clatter into the car park below. There was a mighty cheer as the Cup Final continued with the now added advantage of a football.

"Thanks, Tanker! I'll drop it up after!" promised Dunnzer as Tanker closed the window and Dunnzer put his "microphone" back up to his mouth and began to enthuse about how the crowd were really loving this one.

Tanker didn't go back to sleep. He half-listened to the game outside. The grating rat-a-tat-tat of the can had been replaced by the much more soothing thumpety-thump-thump of the football. The shouting and Dunnzer's expert opinions could also be heard, yet soon Tanker was able to ignore them.

Saturday was a funny day for Tanker. In one way he loved the freedom from school. Second year had been much harder than first and he was constantly being reminded that his Junior Cert was only around the corner. His Christmas report had been terrible. His test results were even worse. One honour, six passes and four fails, with one of those an F in Maths. As mid-term approached, teachers were giving him daily reminders that he had loads of ability but just wasn't putting in the study time. Tanker knew he would have to work harder but time seemed to be slipping by too fast.

He was finding it difficult to know when to actually get started and how. He spent the whole week wishing it was the weekend. Then when the weekend came he realised he had something else to dread. Saturday meant Dad's visit. How he hated that visit.

Tanker got up and made tea. He knew his mother would still be asleep but he brought her in a cup and opened the curtains.

"In the name of God, Thomas, what time is it?" she moaned from beneath the quilt.

"Dunno, Mam. It's about nine." Tanker spoke in a half whisper as he placed the cup beside the bed. "Do you want toast?"

"Do you want to a kick up the backside?"

"What?"

"Thomas, it's the middle of the night. Would you for God's sake close those bloody curtains and get the hell out of here. Bring me a cup of tea about twelve!"

"But, Mam, it's Saturday. Dad's visit?"

"We can go at three."

"But, Mam, you said last week that we could go in the morning this week. You know I hate going in the afternoons."

"Thomas, I'm losing it! Close the door on your way out. Oh and by the way, there's a list of things for your dad on the kitchen table. Take a tenner out of me purse and get them."

"But, Mam!"

"No buts, Thomas! Out!"

That sounded pretty final to Tanker who closed the door as requested behind him.

He threw three sausages on the grill and buttered three slices of toast. The one good thing about Dad not being around was that there was always a bit more food in the flat. When Dad was around he spent most of the day eating. That caused much of the hassle between himself and Mam. That and the "nightwork".

Tanker had never known his dad going to real work. Dad used to joke about "being on nights again this week" and his mother would start whispering out of the corner of her mouth something about "not saying that in front of the child". Tanker knew soon enough what the joke was about. He began to realise also that Dad's long absences were not caused by his going to work in England as his mother used to tell him. School changed all that.

He hardly had dried his eyes on his first morning in junior infants at St Peter's Primary when he heard the taunts.

"Your daddy's a jail-bird!"

"My mam said I'm not to sit next to you cos' your Dad's in jail for all his life and sentence!"

"Your daddy is a murderer and he has a big knife and he'd stick it in ya if ya looked at him!"

"No he's not. My mam said he's an army robber and he'd hold ya up in the bank!"

Why were all these children saying these nasty things? Day after day the teasing continued. In the yard, in the toilets, in the corridors, all the time he was being told things he didn't understand by children who didn't understand what they were saying, but would say them anyway. His mam had told him that Dad had gone to work in England. He was building a bridge in Bristol. He would be back in a year's time. Tanker had no reason to disbelieve his own mother.

Then one day he found out the truth. His mother dressed him up in his cleanest sweatshirt and jeans and brought him to see his father. Maybe it was because of the question he had asked her the night before.

"Mam, what does it mean if you do hard labour?"

"Hard labour? Who used those words to you, Thomas love?" She was taken by surprise.

"A boy in my class said that Dad was doing hard labour and I told him he was wrong, he was building bridges in Bristol."

As it turned out both Tanker and his classmate were wrong. Thomas Kelly Senior was doing eighteen months for petty theft. He was serving his sentence in Cork Prison, a mere twenty minutes walk from Terence MacSwiney Mansions. While young Thomas had been imagining his father building bridges over the River Severn with a giant Mecano set, his father had actually been making light-aircraft models during his woodwork classes in the prison.

The shock of seeing his father in his prison denim blue was one from which Tanker never fully recovered. However, over the next few years it was to be a regular sight, as despite his constant promises to reform, Tanker's dad was to continue to specialise in "nightwork".

Nevertheless, the teasing became easier now that Tanker knew the truth. He was able to silence all the false accusations of murder, armed robbery and assault and battery.

"Me dad does nightwork!" he would inform them. "And sometimes he gets caught!"

Chapter 2

No Disco

"Oh it's you, Tanker. Come in. Yeoman is in the loo. I'll tell him you're here. That is if you want to see him."

"What?" Tanker was confused.

"Maybe it's me you wanted to see?" Celia Dunne was always doing this to Tanker and it always had the same result. He blushed. His cheeks turned so beetroot red they wouldn't have looked out of place in a mixed salad.

"No, Celia... " he was fumbling for words but only sounds were coming. "I er... mm... well... mmm... I... er ... was hoping... er... mm to... mm... see Yeoman!"

"You mean you didn't call to see me!" She loved doing this and Tanker hated it. Celia Dunne was a student nurse in the University Hospital. She was nineteen, slim and beautiful. Tanker was fourteen and a quarter, small, fat and spotty. It just wasn't fair.

"I'll wait in the living room if you don't mind, Celia."

The blush was beginning to fade as he went into the living room. Aidan was there eating an apple and watching a United video.

"Hi, Tanker! Thanks for the ball. I called down to your flat with it but there was nobody there."

"No, me mam and myself went up to see Dad."

"Is he still in?"

"Yeah. He'll be out in a fortnight."

"Yeah... and back in again in a month?" Dunnzer was trying to be funny and failing miserably.

"Eat your bloody apple... "

Tanker wasn't really annoyed. Dunnzer was five years his junior. You didn't get upset with a kid of that age. He looked at the screen.

"Who are they playing?"

"It's the highlights of all their Cup Finals since the Seventies. This is the one against Chelsea. Four-nil. Classic."

"Not if you follow Chelsea!"

Tanker noticed a neat pile of cola ring-pulls on the coffee table.

"How many more do you need, Dunnzer?"

"I've got fifty seven so I need forty three for the ball or I might go for the sweatshirt."

"You need two hundred for that. That'd take years!"

There was a special Premier League promotion on the cans. All the kids in the area, as well as the rest of the country, were frantically trying to build up a stockpile of ring-pulls. Tanker only needed another ten to have enough to get the "Regulation Weight, Limited Edition, Premier League in Conjunction with Coca-Cola, Superball". His friend Joe who ran the local chipper was collecting them for him.

"I'm nearly there. When I'm finished I'll give you the ones Joe collects for me in the chipper!"

"Ah sound man, Tanker!"

"Don't mention it... butthead!"

Yeoman came in with his jacket already on.

"Will we go now, Tanker?"

"Yeah, sure."

If there was one person from whom Tanker was inseparable it was Yeoman. It was Yeoman who had christened him "Tanker". He called him that when they were in infants and young Thomas went through an obsession with Thomas the Tank Engine. Lately Yeoman was tempted to rename his friend, The Fat Controller.

They went everywhere together. Tonight it was the school disco. Tanker hated discos. He hated the noise and flashing lights. He hated not being able to see properly or hear properly. He hated the music and the way people danced. All that bopping up and down and head banging. It made him giddy just to watch. And watching was all he ever did. He would never have the nerve to ask somebody to dance and the chances of being asked himself ranged from a thousand to a million to one.

Yeoman on the other hand was a disco kid. He milked the scene as he strutted his moves on the floor. He knew all the words to the songs which Tanker felt was no great boast as most of them just involved yelling the word "Yah!" on every fourth beat. Yeoman disagreed with his friend claiming the words were hidden in the music.

"It's a feeling from the vibes, Tanker! A sort of energy. It gets you fired up!"

"Energy, my ass, Yeoman. It just gives me a headache!"

Tanker went along all the same as he knew Yeoman appreciated the company. Once they were there Tanker told him he was quite happy to sit with his coke and watch the talent. In truth Tanker would have been a lot happier at home watching the telly or playing his tapes. He felt completely out of it. As he watched Yeoman spelling out the words of a rap song, which involved some guy shooting a cop in Harlem and "doing it for the brothers", Tanker was sorry he didn't stay in Dunne's flat and watch that United video with Dunnzer. He looked at his watch and was dismayed when he realised it was only nine o'clock. Another two hours to go. How was he going to stand it?

He looked around the floor for the remote possibility that there might be a girl he could ask to dance. There wasn't. All the girls without boyfriends were dancing in little circles with their handbags in the middle. There were circles of boys doing the same, although without the array of handbags. Gradually as the dancing progressed the circles began to overlap. Even if he wanted to ask somebody he wouldn't have been able, unless he had joined in one of these circles and endured a couple of hours of head-banging with Yeoman and his rapping pals until they were lucky enough to collide with a similar group of rapping females.

Tanker was tempted to leave. The only thing stopping him was the fear of having to walk back to the Mansions on his own. This was not a wise thing to do after dark. Terence MacSwiney Mansions were situated on the northside of Cork, adjacent to the notorious Magillicuddy Heights. The flat complex had become well known for the gang activity which went on there. Drug pushing had become a major crime. Being mugged for the price of a fix was a regular occurrence. While Tanker had never actually been mugged the thought of it happening to him was a constant fear. Tonight he would wait for Yeoman no matter how long it might take.

"Hi, Tanker! What's up with you?" It was Lucy Higgins. "Nothing, Lu, I just don't like dancing. It makes me feel like a cow on hind legs."

"I know. I'm not into it much either."

"Why did you come?"

"Nothing on the telly on a Friday night. Anyway, it's Mandy's birthday so she wanted us all to go boppin'," she paused, "or in Mandy's case, 'poppin'!"

"How do you mean?" Tanker asked.

Lucy smiled at him. She marvelled at his innocence.

"Never mind, Tanker. Forget it."

"If you like. Do you want to sit down?"

"Sure. How's your dad?"

"Don't ask."

"Sorry, Tanker."

Lucy Higgins was born in St Finbarr's Hospital on the same day as Tanker. She lived next door on the same floor in the same block as him. They went to the same primary school where they sat in the same row each year for eight years. They were now in the same secondary school. They had so much in common that Tanker often thought Lucy might have been his own female form or at the very least his shadow.

Lucy referred to Tanker as her lunar twin while Tanker

– 13 –

privately thought of Lucy as his looney twin. He based his theory on the fact that Lucy was completely off the wall. She lived alone with her mother who read palms for a living. Lucy went out of her way to dress differently. She wore full-length skirts which looked like old curtains and used to wear her hair in a turban before she decided to shave her head. She was now completely bald except for three little beaded dreadlocks, two of which dangled in front of each ear while the third formed an anorexic-looking pony tail. She wore rings on every finger, including thumbs, and bangle-sized earrings jingled every time she moved her head. Her nose was studded on either side and a tattoo of a whale adorned her neck.

Lucy believed in reincarnation and once told Tanker that they were both chariot horses of a Roman Emperor in a previous existence. At times Tanker wished Lucy would somehow return to a previous existence or at least stay out of his present one. She followed horoscopes and claimed she had her mother's gift for reading palms. Tanker, she claimed, would live until he was one hundred and ten and have several wives.

"Your life line is incredible, Tanker! And your love lines! Wow! They look eternal, babe!"

Tanker thought Lucy was slowly losing her marbles, even though part of him wanted to believe that one.

"Got a light?" The voice was both unfamiliar and aggressive.

"Don't smoke," said Tanker flatly, looking up to see who was asking. He saw a tall figure in a zipped-up leather jacket standing over him with a cigarette dangling from his mouth.

"Here," offered Lucy who was not easily intimidated. She flicked her lighter to his unlit cigarette.

"Thanks," he nodded. "Want a smoke?"

"Got me own, thanks." grinned Lucy, waving a box of menthols.

Leather Jacket grinned at her mockingly.

"Much better flavour to these!" He inhaled deeply from his cigarette which looked to Tanker like one of those roll-your-owns which his grandad used to smoke.

Tanker smiled meekly at this stranger, hoping that the silence would provoke him into moving away and annoying somebody else. His first reaction to Leather Jacket was one of dislike. He didn't like that smug grin. He didn't like the way he blew smoke into the air in little rings as if he were sending out smoke signals. Me, big chief leather jacket, you, spotty little fat guy.

Thankfully, as the last of the smoke rings disintegrated into the flashing orange lights overhead, Leather Jacket moved towards the dance floor and began shaking his head from side to side in perfect rhythm to the music.

"Sleazeball!" muttered Tanker under his breath, but loud enough for Lucy to hear.

"Do you know him, Tanker?"

"Never saw him before. I don't think he's from around here."

"He's kind of cute-looking!" Lucy was smirking.

"Cute? What do you mean by that?"

"Cute! You know. Nice. He's got a nice bum!"

"Cut it out, Lu! He's a slime merchant – anyone can see that!"

"Oh don't be so touchy Tanker. I'm only messing. Anyway you've got a nice bum too. Big but nice!"

"I said cut it out, Lu!"

There was an awkward pause as Lucy stared straight ahead and Tanker tried to sneak a look over his shoulder and measure his backside.

"Anyway, since when did you start smoking? Your old one would break your neck if she found out!"

"Oh like, you're going to tell her?"

"Don't be daft!"

"Come on, Tanker." Lucy pulled her next-door neighbour by the hand. "Let's go and pretend we can dance!"

"No thanks, Lu. I'm a crap dancer. You know that. Please. I'd prefer to watch!"

"Oh button it, Tanker! Come on! I'll look after you! And I'll even walk you home after!"

By the time they reached the floor there was a general mingling of both the male and female circles. Basically people were just doing their own thing. Yeoman was apparently trying a duet with Helen O'Sullivan, whom he fancied but hadn't the nerve to ask out yet. The two of them were singing into imaginary mikes which they were holding over their heads and shaking as they screamed out the lyrics which again sounded like an endless repetition of the word "Yah". Tanker swayed his hips as best he could but he couldn't help feeling like a human spinning top. No matter how hard he tried to get into this music it still sounded like listening to a train.

Lu had promised not to abandon him, even though Tanker feared that once she saw what a pathetic dancer she had found herself with she would want to do an on-the-spot disappearing act. Thankfully she had enough after twenty minutes of the endless "Yah" and they sat out the remainder of the night with Tanker thinking about his father's imminent release and Lu giving marks out of ten for any bum that came into view.

Chapter 3

Blood Brothers

Yeoman was feeling sorry for himself all the way home. Helen O'Sullivan had said no. Lucy tried to make light of the situation by telling him that Helen O'Sullivan was to the human race what a ball of pus is to a boil.

"In her previous existence, Yeoman, Helen O'Sullivan was a fly on a cow's bum. I know these things. I'm psychic!"

"Shut it, Lucy!" Yeoman snapped.

"Of course, your royal highness! Sorry for trying to make you feel better. In future I'll try not to be such a good neighbour. Here, you miserable little sod, have a menthol."

Yeoman looked at the packet of cigarettes in Lucy's hand and laughed. "Since when did you start smoking? Your old one will break your neck if she finds out!"

Tanker and Lucy both laughed and said together, "Oh like, you're going to tell her!"

Yeoman didn't get the joke but he smiled anyway. They went into Joe's Diner and ordered chips.

"Tanker, just the man I wanted to see!" Joe Brady rubbed the grease from his fingers as he called Tanker over to the counter for a private word.

"Can you work on Sunday?"

"I dunno, Joe. Me mam hates me working here. You know like, with school on Monday and all that."

"I know but I'm really stuck. Phil's back is playing up again and she could do with a break. Two pounds an hour, five hour shift and you can go at twelve."

"Two-fifty and I'll go at eleven."

"Done!" Joe smiled as he made his way back to the sizzling oil. He liked Tanker. The boy had worked for him the previous school holidays. Joe often asked him in to work when he was stuck for staff, although Tanker's mother wasn't too pleased about his working there. A recent school report wouldn't help his case this time either but Tanker knew the prospect of some extra cash would win her over eventually.

Joe served the three of them himself. He threw in three batter burgers on top of the chips and three cokes and waved them away when they tried to pay.

"On the house! Oh, and here's another few of those coke ring things." He handed Tanker about ten ring-pulls.

"Brilliant, Joe! One 'Regulation Weight, Limited Edition, Premier League in Conjunction with Coca-Cola, Superball' on it's way!"

"See you Sunday, Tanker!"

They took their food to a plastic counter and sat up on three high stools. Lucy was going through a serious anti-meat phase and held up her batter burger in a which-one-of-you-wants-this style. The anti-meat phase had developed from her serious vegetarian phase.

"Anti-meat is strong. It's a statement. Like *'I do not approve of the killing of poor defenseless animals'*. Meat is murder!" she explained for about the hundredth time as Tanker and Yeoman both made a grab at the spare burger tearing it in half.

"Have neither of you heard of Mad Cow Disease?"

They looked at her quizzically.

"I think I'm looking at a mad cow!" laughed Yeoman.

Lucy eyeballed Yeoman with an icy stare. A stare which demanded an instant apology.

"Sorry, Lucy! Only joking!"

"As I was saying," she continued her lecture, "meat is murder. Cold-blooded, throat-slitting murder. Both of you are assisting in the destruction of the universe as we know it. Non-human cannibalism. Both of you are adding to the slaughter of a poor defenceless animal."

"Lucy, eat your chips and let myself and Tanker devour

this poor defenceless batter-burger! Hey, Tanker, I suppose that's why they call them batter burgers, they were battered to death!" Yeoman laughed at his own joke while Lucy glared. If they weren't going to listen to reasonable points it was time for a short sharp shock.

"You wouldn't laugh if you knew what part of the animal they use for burger meat!" she told them. Both Tanker and Yeoman stopped eating and stared at their food. For a moment they considered not finishing the burgers until hunger won them over and they gobbled away ravenously. Lucy knew when she was beaten. She threw her eyes up to heaven and sipped her coke.

"Hi!" The voice was familiar and so were the smoke rings.

"Oh, hi there, Denis!" Yeoman smiled as he greeted the Leather Jacket. "Are you getting something?"

"No, I just picked up a take-away."

"Do you want to join us?"

"No thanks, Yeoman. I've a cab waiting outside. See you on Monday!"

Tanker stared as the smoke rings made an exit out of the diner. They seemed to be saying, "You're right, spotty face! I am a sleazeball!"

"Who is he, Yeoman?"

"Oh, he's a new fella in fifth year. I got talking to him on Friday in detention. He was thrown out of his last school."

"He said he had a cab waiting outside! A cab! Who in the name of God can afford to travel in taxis around here?" Tanker was baffled.

"He's not from around here, Tanker. He's from Cnoc Barra. No other school would take him, only St Peter's."

"Cnoc Barra? He's from Cnoc Barra? You have to be kidding!" Tanker couldn't take this in. His perception of Cnoc Barra was of an area of huge houses protected by perimeter fencing, surveillance cameras, rottweilers and burglar alarms. How could anybody from Cnoc Barra end up in St Peter's?"

"In a previous existence," Lucy was at it again, "our friend Leather Jacket was an Egyptian pharoah who had maids feeding him grapes while he bathed in asses' milk!"

"Egyptian pharoah, my ass! Egyptian fairy more like! Did you see the way he had his hair slicked back with oil? And that leather jacket! He looks like a right eejit if you ask me!" Tanker was making his dislike public.

"No you're wrong there, Tanker. Denis is cool!" Yeoman stated quite matter-of-factly.

"Cool?" Tanker nearly fell of his stool. "Cool? Yeoman, has Helen O'Sullivan blowing you out tonight affected your active brain cell count? The guy is a walking butt-head! A prize sleaze!"

"Ah, you only think that, Tanker. He comes across as a bit of a know-all at first. But once you get to know him he's grand."

Tanker eyed Yeoman suspiciously. Yeoman had never mentioned Denis up to now and he was supposed to be his best friend. More than that, they were blood brothers. They had made a secret pact when they were eight never to have secrets from each other. They both made their fingers bleed with the aid of a compass and smudged their initials at the end of a note declaring that "Thomas Kelly (Tanker) and Eamon Dunne (Yeoman) are now officially blood relations. Together forever." Tanker had seen it done in a western where the note was actually written in blood drawn from self-inflicted knife wounds. Neither of them wanted to risk that so Tanker just pierced a wart with the compass while Yeoman bravely nipped the top of his thumb. After seven years the pact now seemed in danger of collapsing. Tanker felt totally dismayed.

"Why did you not mention him before, Yeoman?" he asked as they finished the last of their chips.

"Who, Denis?"

"Yeah, Denis!" Tanker spat the name out as if it was as sour as his last vinegar-soaked chip.

"I forgot about him. I only ever spoke to him a few times, but he's a nice enough guy. Like I told you, he's sound."

"Yeah, but you never said anything about him up to now. You should have told me!"

Yeoman gave Tanker a cynical stare. A sort of who-do-you-think-you-are? stare. Tanker had never seen that look on his friend's face before and it stung.

"Why should I tell you, Tanker? I don't have to tell you everything, do I?" Yeoman threw his eyes up to heaven and sniggered. At that point Tanker was going to remind him of the pact, the yellowing note that he kept in his bedroom between the mattress and the base of his bed. But there was no point. Yeoman would probably give him that stare again and tell him not to be so childish. Tanker felt totally dejected, almost betrayed.

The three walked home together, keeping an eye out for any would-be muggers. Only Lucy spoke. She told them she was going through a Parisian phase.

"The French are so stylish, don't you think?"

Her question went unanswered so she just carried on about her love for croissants which she had learned to bake and how she would only drink café au lait now. Yeoman said goodnight and left Lucy and Tanker on the fourth floor as he made his way up to the fifth.

"See ya, Tanker!" Lucy smiled as she turned the key in the door of her flat.

Tanker just nodded at her as he opened his own door.

"Don't be upset, Tanker. Yeoman didn't mean it. He can be a bit of a jerk at times. You know the way it is. Probably executed for a crime he didn't commit in a previous existence. It might have left him bitter. Every now and then he gets angry about it. Hard to blame him."

"Yeah, I suppose, Lu. Only... "

"What?"

Tanker shook his head and waved goodnight. Once inside he finished the sentence for himself.

" ...the pact is over. Goodbye blood brothers."

Chapter 4

Good Behaviour

When he heard the banging on the door Tanker was convinced that they were having a break-in. A quick glance at his clock told him it was seven o'clock in the morning.

"God almighty! Who the hell is that at this hour?" He ran into his mother's room as he struggled to pull up his jeans.

"Mam! Wake up! There's someone trying to get in!"

Ann Kelly would sleep through an earthquake.

"Go away, Tanker!" she moaned as she pulled the pillows from under her and put them over her head. "Bring me a cup of tea around eleven! There's a good boy now!"

"Mam! Seriously! There's somebody breaking down the door!"

Tanker picked up his baseball bat and made his way to the door. He put on his most threatening voice.

"Who is it?"

"Tanker, for crying out loud, will you open the bloody door! It's me! Your father! I've no key! Will you open the door?"

"Dad?" Tanker sighed with relief as he unbolted the door top and bottom and turned the key in the main lock.

"Christ, Dad, you're not on the run, are you?" There was something about his father that always made Tanker fear the worst. Here was his father home, after spending the past year behind bars, and all Tanker could think of was how he made good his escape.

"On the run? Of course I am, Tanker! That's why I came here. The last place the guards would think of looking would be me own flat!" Tanker's suspicious mind was not lost on his father who in return gave his usual display of sarcasm.

"Those nail files are a great job. I was able to burrow a tunnel all the way from me cell to the corner of the estate. I made friends with a rabbit on the way. Nice chap. Fella by the name of Bugs Bunny. Big teeth. Eats a lot of carrots. Claims he has his own show on the telly. Do you know him?"

"Dad!" Tanker snapped. After the fright he had suffered on wakening, he wasn't ready for his father's weird sense of humour. "What are you doing home so early?"

"Are you going to let me in to me own flat?"

"Sorry!" Tanker stood to one side to allow his father in.

"You're asking me why I'm home so early. I could ask you where you intend playing baseball at this hour of the morning!"

Tanker looked at the baseball bat he was still holding. He put it down as he mumbled something about thinking that his father was an intruder.

"In the name of God, Tanker, who would want break in here. There's nothing worth taking. Apart from your mother. By the way, where is your mother?"

At that moment Tom Kelly Senior's question was answered as Ann Kelly came out of the bedroom and stared in disbelief at her husband.

"Jesus... Tom Kelly! What are you doing here?"

"Isn't that a lovely welcome home greeting!" Tom Kelly shook his head.

"You didn't escape, did you?"

"Holy mother of divine mercy, give me strength! Another one!"

"Well?" Ann continued to stare.

"They let me out at six. There was a big gang of dealers brought in last night on remand. The governor was called in and he decided to leave ten of us go. The good behaviour gang! Model prisoner number FB7 02367, that's me! Sure I only had another two weeks left anyway. Where's the big deal?"

Mother and son looked at each other. Tanker nodded an I-believe-him nod and his mother seemed to agree.

"Tanker, put the kettle on. Make your old man and meself a cup of tea. Put on some toast too."

"Toast, my backside! I want a big fry with two runny eggs and half a dozen sausages. The only fry I had inside was on Christmas day and you could have used the yolk of the egg as a cue-ball!"

Ann Kelly sighed and then smiled. Her husband may have been insufferable but he could always make her laugh. For short periods of time at least. He followed her into the kitchen as she told Tanker to leave it, that she would fix breakfast. Tanker felt better that his father was home even though he knew that soon he would start worrying as to when he would be whisked away again. He could feel himself beginning to worry about the rows too. How long would the merriment last before one of those would begin?

"That's it anyway. Never again. I'm never again going to put one foot inside that place!"

The announcement came as Tom Kelly wiped the last traces of runny yolk from his plate with a slice of bread. This was not the first time he had made such an announcement, therefore neither Tanker nor his mother took much notice.

"Tommy, you always say that. Every time you get released you come home, demand a fry, eat the fry and then tell us you're going straight."

"I mean it this time," he insisted as he took a cigarette from his wife's box and lit one. She glared at him.

"Sorry!" He picked up the box again and pushed it towards her. "Would the lady like a cigarette?"

She snatched the box from him and sighed as she lit her own.

"No, I definitely mean it this time. There was a time when thieving was an art form. I saw meself as a self-styled Robin Hood. Stealing from the rich... "

"And giving to yourself... " added Tanker before his father

had a chance to finish the sentence.

"Don't be cheeky, young Tanker! As I was saying, I stole from the rich to give to the poor who, as it turned out, happened to be meself."

Tanker laughed out loud. He had heard this Robin Hood theory hundreds of times. It was his father's attempt to justify his "trade".

"It's different nowadays, though. When I thieve, correction, when I *thieved,* I never hurt anybody. I never carried arms, except for me trusty screwdriver which I only ever used on screws. I never broke into a house that was occupied and I always tidied up after meself! I often left a letter of apology in certain circumstances..."

"That's enough, Tom! Joke's over!" Ann Kelly got up from the table and started shaking her fist at her husband. "Shut your stupid mouth right now in front of the boy!"

"Take it easy, Ann!"

"Don't you take-it-easy-Ann me!"

"For God's sake, woman, cool it!"

"Don't you dare tell me to cool it, you good-for-nothing waster!"

"Ann, please, not in front of... !"

"Oh, so you don't like the boy hearing his father called a waster?"

"Ann!" Thomas Kelly couldn't possibly stop her now. She was in full flight.

"Okay so, Tanker, son. Your father is a maggot, a parasite, a spineless cheat, a scumbag and, above all, a jailbird!"

"Stop it, Ann! Ann, please!" The more he begged her to stop the more incensed she became.

"Don't you ever again try and tell us that what you do is not too bad and all that crap! You are as pathetic a criminal as those coke-heads and dope-fiends you despise so much! So don't you ever try to fool my son into believing that you are any different! Because you're not! You're just the same!

A low-life! Do you hear that! A good for nothing low-life!"

Tanker hated this. One minute they were having a laugh together as a family the next she explodes. His dad was only trying to explain that not all criminals were the same. That he wasn't into drugs and violence. That he wasn't into hurting anybody. That crime had changed and that from now on he wasn't going to get involved in it any more. And what happens? She has to suddenly explode! It just wasn't fair. The three of them were only back together half an hour and already she was causing a fight, saying he was no better than a junkie, no different to the crack-pots and coke-heads. That was untrue. He was better than them. A hell of a lot better.

"Just leave me out of this one!" Tanker yelled. He banged his fist on the table, knocking over a cup as he left the kitchen and ran into his bedroom. "Why can't the two of you just... "

"Tanker!" his father called after him.

"Leave him go!"

Tanker heard their row continue as he lay on his bed with his pillow pulled tight against his ears. Muffled words like "spoil", "ruin", "go to hell", "different this time", "promise", "a real job" and "heard it all before", kept coming through and were repeated over and over again as the battle reached a crescendo before it wavered and began to fade. Shouting gave way to speaking and then the calm of the ensuing silence broken only by the odd single word. The row was over. For now.

Tanker lay still. Tears began to well up inside him. He hated that. He was nearly fifteen years old. He should have been able to give up crying years ago but here he was blubbering over his mother and father having a row. All parents argued, didn't they? Why should he feel he was so different? But he did feel different. It all seemed so unfair. Outside it was starting up again.

"I was only trying to tell him that things are different now." His father's voice seemed to plead. "People don't thieve like me any more! It's all robbery with assault. Old people getting hammered by thugs for a few quid they call life savings! I'd never do anything like that! Those people have no feelings! I just wanted the boy to know that his old man isn't one of those!"

Her voice wasn't raised. It seemed sad this time and not as angry.

"But you *are* one of those! Just because you don't hit anybody doesn't make it right! You're a fool, Tom Kelly! A damned fool!"

The words hurt both father and son. There was silence for a while. Another sort of calm-after-the-storm feeling. Tanker pulled the pillow from his ears and sighed as his tears began to subside. The silence was broken by the sound of a match being struck. He thought he heard the word "sorry" being softly spoken. He hoped to God that he did. He could hear his father muttering "thanks" and then blowing out heavily, having taken a long draw on his cigarette. More silence followed as he pictured them both sitting at the table, each avoiding the other's eyes. Both hurters. Both feeling hurt.

Suddenly there was the sound of a chair being moved away from the table and then plates being scraped.

"I'll do that later!"

"No, it's okay. I'll do it. It's been ages since this old fool washed up."

Chapter 5

Yeoman's Return

When he called that Sunday afternon, Yeoman was surprised.

"Hi, Mr Kelly! What are you doing out?"

"Don't you bloody well start!"

"Sorry, but I thought you had another... "

"I escaped!"

Tom Kelly was drinking a cup of tea while watching the omnibus edition of *Eastenders*. He sighed out loud every time somebody in the programme suggested "have a nice cup of tea" raising his own cup and adding in an assumed Cockney accent, "No thanks, love, I've already brewed up!" His wife was doing some mindless questionnaire entitled "How Well Do You Know Your Lover?" in the *News of the World*. She read some of the questions to him

"'If your lover won a thousand pounds, would he/she (a) put it in the bank? (b) spend it on a surprise holiday for you both? (c) not tell you?' Well?"

Tom stared straight ahead at the television.

"Well what?"

"What would you do?"

"I dunno... I don't have a lover!"

She sighed and told him she didn't know what to make of him and continued the earth-shattering survey without his assistance. Tanker consoled himself that this morning's row was over or at least put on hold. It always amazed him how they could do that. One minute screaming and roaring, the next sitting there as if nothing had happened. Nevertheless, he was relieved that for the moment the atmosphere was calm and that they were on speaking terms. Well, sort of anyway.

Things had calmed down since the morning bust-up. His

mother and father hadn't said much but when he offered to go to mass with her she didn't say no. Tanker never remembered seeing his father going to mass before and smiled when he told him that it was just another bad habit he had picked up in the prison. Tanker lied that he had been the night before. This had become the weekly lie. Tanker was sure his mother knew he didn't go to church but he was still afraid to tell her. He preferred it this way. He was sure by the way she asked that she knew. Maybe she preferred it that way too.

It was a relief when they came home from the church together. Tanker's mother normally went to see her own mother in Thomas Davis Street after Sunday mass, while Tanker got the lunch ready, but obviously she was making an exception today. He hoped that this was a good sign.

"What time is your match?" asked Yeoman.

"Four in Kilbarry."

"I think I'll go with you!"

Tanker thought he was hearing things. Yeoman was a strictly Sky Sports Sunday afternoon soccer fan. He would only watch a game if he could hear opinions from a panel of experts and see multi-angle action replays of every near miss. Tanker played in goals for Blackpool Rovers. As far as he could recall, Yeoman had never seen him play before.

Discos? Yes. Raves? Sure. Helen O'Sullivan. Absolutely.

Watching Tanker? Absolutely not. However, Tanker wasn't in the mood to start ridiculing his friend's motives. He was just glad to see him.

"Who are you playing?"

"I'm not sure. Some new club. They're division two but this is a cup match. We've never played them before but they're supposed to be good."

"Blackpool Rovers and St Bonaventure's. Youth Cup semi-final. Kilbarry Pitch two. Four o'clock. Referee Paul Murphy." Tanker's Dad informed them as he continued to stare at

Eastenders. They all looked at him as if he had sprouted an extra nose.

"I memorised all the fixtures and results inside. It gave me something to do. Stopped me from getting bored! And if this programme doesn't end soon I think I'll start memorising them again."

Ann Kelly put her newspaper down.

"Why don't you go to the match with the boys? Tanker would like that, wouldn't you, son?"

"Great. No sweat. Only cool it down on the line, Dad. Last time you went to a game you had to be dragged off the linesman."

"I only told him where he should try waving his flag. Off-side, me foot. We'd have won that bloody match if he'd have been watching it instead of scratching his backside. Anyway, I think I'll give it a miss today. I'll only have every Tom, Dick and Harrietta asking me did I escape!"

"Ah, stop feeling sorry for yourself. I'll go with you if you need a bodyguard. You two boys go on ahead. I'll walk up later on with your father."

Tanker was thrilled to hear his mother saying this. He was able to put the morning's row out of his mind and concentrate on the game. And with Yeoman going along as well it appeared that all his worries were evaporating before his eyes.

Blackpool Rovers 4 St Bonaventures 0. That result should have had Tanker ecstatically happy. When he left the pitch that evening all he wanted to do was to go home and forget. He was furious with Yeoman.

On the way to the game Tanker was convinced that Yeoman was full of remorse for his behaviour the night before. That was why he was going to the game. As a way of saying sorry for being such a prat. However, once on the pitch Tanker realised that his friend may have had an ulterior motive for attending his first open air football match. Centre forward for the opposition was none other than super butt-head, Leather Jacket.

The only satisfaction Tanker derived from the game was saving the penalty. He had given the kick away himself as Leather Jacket rose to head a corner and Tanker thumped him on the back of the head with a double fist. It cost him a yellow card but he would have gladly accepted a life-time ban.

After the game Yeoman informed Tanker that he was taking a lift home from Denis's old man. Tanker looked over to where a large black BMW with alloy sports wheels and tinted windows was parked.

"We're all heading into town for a bite. You're quite welcome to join us, kid!" Denis blew a smoke ring as he offered Tanker the invite.

Tanker wanted to tell him that if he ever called him "kid" again he would break both his legs. However, the violence wouldn't come. Instead he found himself being polite.

"No thanks. I need the air. Anyway, I've got to work in Joe's tonight."

"Okay, Tanker, see you around, kid! You had a great game today! Well done."

Tanker still wanted to break his legs but he found himself nodding and saying "Thanks a lot".

He walked away as Yeoman and Denis sped off in the BMW Denis was driving. His father was in the passenger seat grimacing. Tanker whispered the word "asshole" as the car disappeared through the gates of the ground.

"Some car, eh, Tank?" It was Lucy. She never missed a game.

Tanker grunted his disapproval.

"Big bloody deal!"

"Not a lot of guys get to drive a car like that."

"It's his dad's car! The sleazeball is showing off. Who the

hell does he think he is, Little Lord Fauntleroy?"

"Still, there are lots of kids in the flats who drive BMWs." said Lu as she walked alongside him. Tanker looked at her blankly.

"Except they generally belong to other people's daddys!"

Tanker laughed and told Lucy she was a headcase. Lucy smiled back and told him to cheer up.

"It'll be better in the next life, Tanker! You wait and see!" They sat on a low wall over looking the carpark and watched Aidan Dunne and his friends re-playing the FA Cup Final, which had obviously ended in a draw the day before. They were playing with a ball this time as opposed to the choice of beer and coke cans which littered the car park. The aftermath of the previous night's cider party. Tanker felt a bit silly now for not accepting the lift from Denis.

"Heh, Tanker!" shouted Aidan. "Did Blackpool win?"

"Four-nil!"

"Brilliant! Did you play well?"

"Okay!"

"He was man of the match. In a previous existence he was an octopus!" Lucy chipped in

"Do you want to go on goals here? We're short one!"

Immediately "Liverpool" launched an angry objection.

"He can't play!"

"He's too big!"

"Get lost, Dunnzer!"

"You can't do that, Dunnzer!"

"I told you! I can do what I like!"

Tanker and Lucy got up and headed back to the flats while the United and Liverpool players continued to battle it out.

"Fancy some herbal tea? It's good for stress!"

"No thanks, Lu. I'd better check in with the folks."

"Things will be okay, Tommy!"

Tanker always got worried when Lucy called him that. It wasn't the word so much as the way she said it. Like she was the only one who could pronounce it that way. Like it was her private pet name that only she had permission to use. There were times when he wasn't quite sure whether Lucy wanted to be more than just a good friend. There were times, especially in recent weeks, when he wasn't quite whether he wanted something more himself.

They were both watching an old movie when he came in. It was a western with John Wayne. Tanker's father made room for him on the couch as he pointed to his hero on the screen.

"*True Grit!* One of Wayne's best! He got an Oscar for this one. Greatest cowboy of them all, he was, Tanker!"

"Besides yourself, Dad!"

"Don't be cheeky!"

"Sorry, Dad. Anyway he took care of the wild west. You're a northside cowboy!"

Tanker's mother sniggered as they watched the rest of the film in silence.

Chapter 6

The Perfect Chipper

Tanker's spirits had greatly improved as he served up copious helpings of cod and chips in Joe's Diner. Although from the outside it resembled any other greasy chipper, "Joe's" had gained a reputation for the best fish and chips in Cork. Joe was often featured on radio and television foodie type programmes where he always steadfastly refused to give away the secret to his wonderful deep fried fare.

In truth there was no mystery. Joe used the most expensive cooking oil, had separate friers for fish, sausages, burgers and chips and cleaned each, putting in fresh oil daily. However he often claimed to have secret recipes for batter and methods of producing the perfect chip.

His claims to perfection were well received. Customers came from all over the city to buy chips in "Joe's". From tea-time onwards a steady stream of customers would flow until after midnight when the last of the pub crowd would leave, their beer bellies topped up with cholesterol.

"Five singles, three smoked cod, two batter burgers, a sausage, mushy peas, carton of curry... nine pounds forty please... and yours is on the way... yes I know... four singles three with sauce, vinegar and salt, one salt only, a half a bag with salt and vinegar, no sauce, three fresh hake, one smoked and a bag of onion rings... !"

Tanker loved the challenge of getting the orders right first go. He rarely forgot an item and was able to rattle off the order, to the amazement of the customer, when handing over the food. That was one of the reasons why Joe liked him working there.

This particular Sunday night Tanker seemed to be quicker than ever. Although business was brisk his speed had kept the queue down to a minimum. At half past ten things quietened down and Tanker joined Joe at a table for a coke before the closing time rush. He was telling Joe about his day. He told him about his father coming home but didn't mention the row.

"So I bet your mother is pleased to have him home, is she?"

"I don't know, Joe. I think she was getting used to it just being myself and herself."

"So it's a bit like starting all over again, eh?"

"A bit."

"Don't be surprised if there's a bit of tension for a while, Tanker. Nerves might get a bit frayed."

"Yeah?"

Tanker was amazed at how much Joe seemed to know.

"My wife was in hospital last year. Disc problems. She was in for six months. I couldn't wait for her to be discharged. It was the longest six months of my life. Spending my days up in the Orthopaedic and my nights running this place. Then when she finally came home she drove me around the bend. I used to wish she'd slip another disc and go back into hospital. It's to do with territory, Tanker. We get used to our own space. Then when somebody else comes along into that territory we find it hard to accept. I was so used to being on my own I resented my own wife!"

Tanker smiled.

"Heh, Joe, you sound like David Attenborough! You'll be in his next series. *The Amazing Life of Chip Shops!*"

"Seriously, Tanker, that's what'll happen with your mam and dad. She's going to need time to adjust to having him around and he's going to have to get used to being in a room without somebody locking the door behind him!"

Joe was spot on there. Tanker had noticed that. Things that he would take for granted were a big deal to his father. Like going to the loo. Tanker would just go when he needed. His father would make an announcement. Almost looking for permission like a child in class. "Can I go to the toilet, please Miss?" Only he would say, "I think I need to go the jacks!" Then he would look at his wife or Tanker as if they had to give their blessing first.

The doorbell would startle him too. After not hearing it for months that "ding dong" must have been deafening. When Yeoman had called during *Eastenders* his father almost jumped to attention on hearing it.

Joe was right. They all needed time to adjust. Things would sort themselves out. Soon they would all be back to normal. They would be a proper family again. His father would stay out of trouble. He knew he had broken his promise before but it would be different this time. He believed his father this time.

Tanker headed off home with twelve quid in his pocket at a quarter to twelve. He would have stayed on to help Joe with the last of the pub crowd but Joe's wife Phil came down to relieve him from the upstairs flat where they lived.

"Are you sure you'll be okay walking home?"

"No sweat, Joe. It's only up the road."

"All the same there's a lot of muggings going on. I'll watch you through the window."

"Thanks, Joe. See you. See you, Phil!"

"Goodnight, Tanker! I enjoyed the rest tonight!"

"No problem. Mind your back now!"

As he left the chipper he caught a glimpse in the window of Phil giving Joe one of those "What have you been saying?" stares but he was sure Joe could handle it. Any fellow who could fool half of Cork into believing that his was the best chippie in the country could surely convince his wife that he hadn't been talking about her.

Tanker sprinted home. He felt safe on the main Blackpool Road as there were plenty of people around after the pubs. It was the lane into the flats he hated. He had to pass

MacGillicuddy Heights which he dreaded. He was convinced it was full of winos and junkies. Then again, some of his friends from the Heights thought the same about Terence MacSwiney Mansions. Luckily there were no would-be muggers lurking around the Heights tonight. Not that Tanker spent much time looking. Once past the Heights he came into his own estate. He always felt safe here. He ran up the concrete steps and along the open landing to the door of his flat. Made it.

His father was sitting at the kitchen table reading a book.

"Where's Mam?"

"She's asleep."

"Is everything okay, Dad?"

His father jerked his head sideways. Tanker wasn't sure whether it was a yes nod or a no shake. Maybe something in between.

"What, Dad?"

"What do you mean 'what'?"

"I mean what I asked? Is everything okay?"

"It won't happen like that, son. I've got a lot to prove."

Tanker poured himself a tea and sat down across the table from his father.

"Don't sit there, son," his father said softly.

"But I always sit here. It's me seat!"

His father dropped his eyes. Tanker immediately knew what he meant. His father was tired of people sitting across from him.

"Sorry, Dad. It must make you feel like visiting time. I'll sit next to you!"

"No, no, son. Stay where you are. I've got to get used to things. And I will."

"I know you will, Dad!"

"I mean it, son! No more Robin Hood!" This time there was no laughter in his voice. He wasn't telling it like the fairytale, casting himself in the lead role of robber of the rich and giver to the poor. His voice seemed weak as if he was gasping for breath in order to vocalise. Woven into his words were feelings of shame. Try as he might he couldn't prevent the tears which followed. They flowed down his cheeks like guilty rivers.

He looked across at his son as he wiped his face with the back of his hand. It was hard for Tanker to watch his father crying. He had never seen him cry before. As he watched he surprised himself by not feeling inclined to join in.

"I'm sorry, son!"

Tanker got up and put his arm around his father who fought his tears, sniffing hard and breathing heavily.

"It'll be okay, Tanker, you'll see! It will be different this time!"

"I know, Dad."

Chapter 7

Monday Ten-Thirty am... Bomb Scare?

Tanker would never be able to forgive Seamus Heaney for winning the 1996 Nobel Prize for Literature. Up to then English poetry hadn't been terribly high on his agenda. But now there was no escape. It seemed that every English teacher in the country had gone into Seamus Heaney overdrive. One or two of his poems were easy enough to follow. There was this sad one about his brother dying which Tanker liked. But Miss Lehane wasn't satisfied with those ones. Those were for the weaker students. She wanted them to embark on the "Heaney Challenge".

"Now, we have done several of the easier poems, I'd like you to read this one from Heaney's 1991 collection *Seeing Things*!"

"Ah, Miss, I hate poems!"

"Please, Miss, can we read a short story instead?"

"Please, Miss, this Heaney stuff is crap!"

"Let's talk Liverpool instead, Miss!"

Miss Lehane wasn't ruffled by the negative vibes from Class 2B. Although painfully immersed in her subject she also had expert knowledge of the Premier League which made her hugely popular with the boys in the class. As a keen Liverpool supporter she often held class discussions on games played the previous weekend. Yeoman had christened her "The Babe" and reckoned that one day she would run away with him. Tanker could understand fully why his friend had given her this nickname although he was always careful not to use it in front of Lucy who used to freak out when Yeoman called her that.

"As I said, read the poem quietly and analyse it for theme. Note the structure... "

"Ah, Miss, tell us about the time you went out with John Barnes instead!"

"I did not go out with John Barnes!"

"You told us you did!"

"After the final against Villa!"

"I was in the same hotel bar and I had my photograph taken with him!"

"But you were sitting on his lap, Miss!"

"Yeah, you showed us the picture! You had your scarf around both your necks!"

"It was just a laugh! A photo!"

Class 2B had her sidetracked. Once she got into Liverpool and the Cup Final she was cornered. There was no way back for Seamus Heaney now!

"It must have been dead romantic, Miss!" Lucy was joining in. No doubt she would bring up John Barnes' previous existence as some African prince.

"I did not go out with John Barnes!"

"Ah now, Miss! We all saw the photo! You were all over him!"

"After it was taken he went off with the rest of the team for a meal! That was all. Now as I was saying, read the poem."

"It must have been brilliant, Miss. Being there, seeing them win, meeting the players..." Yeoman was determined to keep her at Wembley.

"Yes, it was, Eamon, but we've only twenty minutes left so could you please read the poem..."

She stopped in mid-sentence as the school alarm bell sounded three times. Fire drill.

"Great!" whispered Tanker to Lu as they got up to leave.

"Okay folks! You know the score!"

"Three-two, Miss, after extra time!"

"Don't be smart, Eamon! Leave everything behind and make your way to the yard. Line up for a head count on the volleyball sideline!"

Fire drills were regularly held. At least once a term. Everybody knew that there wasn't a real fire. In a real fire situation nobody would be so calm. It would be a case of everybody for himself and a massive stampede. Still, as far as Tanker was concerned, it was a welcome relief from Seamus Heaney.

The yard was full of students within a minute. Mr Greene, or Greenfly as he was more affectionately known, would probably tell them over the intercom that they were two minutes down on the last drill and would need to move more quickly the next time. He always said that. By Tanker's calculations that would have meant it had taken them ten and a half minutes to get to the yard. In the event of a real fire he reckoned everybody would be out in ten and a half seconds. This morning, however, old Greenfly was not too concerned with timing the evacuation.

"Good morning!" His voice coming over the intercom hushed the buzzing of student conversations in the yard. He always sounded as if was choking on a hard-boiled sweet. From the worried tone of his voice this morning Tanker was sure he had tried to swallow a whole packet.

"The school will remain closed for the next two hours due to a bomb scare."

The message was greeted with a mighty cheer from the yard. Tanker was a little confused. There was something about the way he had said the last two words which made Tanker feel that his principal wasn't being totally honest with his students. Bomb scare! Who would want to bomb St Peter's? Apart from eight hundred students, he couldn't think of anyone having a motive for bombing the school. No way was there a bomb in the school!

"Hey, Yeoman! A bomb! What do you... ?"

But Yeoman was already back at the main door of the school where he was arguing with Dopey Dick the caretaker.

"What's up with Yeoman?" he asked Lucy.

"Don't know. He muttered something about leaving his

money in his jacket. So what do you think, Tanker? Are we going to get nuked?"

"Bomb, my ass. Greenfly must think we've been transported to Belfast. Come on, Lu, let's go and get some breakfast. I had none this morning and I'm bloody starved. I'll just give Yeoman a shout."

Tanker made his way back to the main door where Yeoman was having a war with Dopey Dick.

"Listen! For the millionth time, I just want me jacket!"

"No way! Orders is orders! The doors are locked and they are staying locked."

"God almighty! It's no wonder they call you Dopey! You can't even follow a simple sentence!"

Dopey Dick was not provoked by Yeoman's insult. He stood defiantly with his arms folded across his chest and his back to the locked doors.

"Come on, Yeoman boy! I've got money, you don't need your jacket!"

Yeoman mouthed the word "dickhead" under his breath as he followed Tanker and Lucy towards the gates.

They went in to a small cafe across from the school. Tanker ordered two jumbo sausage sandwiches and three cups of tea. He had given most of his money from working in the chipper the night before to his mother but he had just enough left to pay. Lucy was still on her anti-meat diet. Thank God for that, thought Tanker, as he put his last fifty pence into his pocket.

Yeoman was still moaning about his jacket as he ploughed his way through his sandwich.

"If that jacket is missing I'll fix that Dopey Dick!"

"And who's going to take it, Yeoman? One of the guards?"

"It might look good on Greenfly," suggested Lucy. "I always saw him as a denim and chains man myself!"

"Shut it, Lu!"

There was silence as Lucy sipped her tea and Tanker and Yeoman munched hungrily.

Tanker couldn't quite accept the bomb scare theory.

"It just doesn't add up," he said out of the blue as if the others were tuned into his mind.

"What?" asked Yeoman through a mouthful of sausage, bread and ketchup.

"The guards searching for a bomb. I mean who in the name of God would want to blow up St Peter's?"

Nobody commented. He turned to Lucy for support.

"What do you think, Lu?"

"I think anybody who eats a sausage should return in the next life as a pig!" Lucy was still in her serious anti-meat mood. "Do either of you realise how pigs are slaughtered?"

Tanker shook his head.

"Do you realise which part of the pig they use in the making of sausages? Or should I have said which parts?"

"Shut it, Lu'!" Tanker put his sandwich down and drank his tea. Lucy may have been a total headcase but this anti-meat thing of hers was having the desired effect. Yeoman, however, had obviously not being listening to her.

"Are you eating that?" Yeoman asked hungrily.

Tanker shook his head and Yeoman grabbed the remains of his sausage sandwich and wolfed it down as if he only had seconds to live.

"Yeoman," Lucy sighed as she watched Yeoman lick his lips like a satisfied cat, "in a previous existence you were a vulture!"

"Yeah, Lucy, and you were definitely someone's cranky granny! Come on, let's go back and see what's happening."

"What's the rush?" asked Tanker. Greenfly said two hours. We've only been here ten minutes. Besides, they give you a free top-up of hot tea here and mine's gone cold."

"Mine too!" added Lucy.

"Well I'm heading back now anyway just to see what's going on. See you later!"

"What's his hurry?" asked Lucy. "Anybody would think there was a fire the way he rushed out of here!"

Chapter 8

Exam Fever

The fire drill or bomb scare was a hoax. Not a hoax in the way that all fire drills are hoaxes, but a hoax deliberately organised by the gardaí to swoop on the locker room. They had suspected various students of being involved in drug pushing and evacuating the building seemed a perfect opportunity to catch these pushers by surprise.

However, the plan appeared to have backfired. Apart from a few dodgy porno magazines and the odd packet of cigarette tobacco they found nothing. The students were rewarded for their patience by receiving the rest of the day off.

Greenfly made the short announcement on the intercom and asked all students to return to the main building and take their coats and belongings home. Tanker checked his locker which didn't seem to have been disturbed at all. It contained nothing other than a corned beef sandwich and bundle of books. If the gardaí had searched it they had certainly done so neatly.

"I see nobody nicked your jacket!" he said as he saw Yeoman standing beside him with his hands deep in the pockets of his favourite piece of denim.

"Thank God for that." Yeoman looked relieved as he spoke. "Come on, Tank, let's go and have a game of snooker."

"Nah. I think I'll head home."

"Ah come on, Tanker, the league starts in three weeks' time. We need all the practice we can get."

"And the exams are on next week, Yeoman!"

Tanker decided to spend the rest of the day studying. This would be day one of Operation Catch Up Fast. Yeoman wanted to join him but Tanker reckoned that they would only start messing around and would probably end up heading off for a game of snooker after half an hour. They struck a compromise. They would both study on their own for three hours and then go for a game of snooker. Lucy said she would study on her own too but if any of them needed a hand to call around to her place. After twenty minutes trying to solve some mathematical theorems Tanker found that he needed that hand.

Lucy made herbal tea and gave him some wholemeal biscuits as she set about drawing diagrams.

"It's all commonsense, Tanker. Logic. A implies B which in turn implies C. Take for example Pythagoras' Theorem. The square on the hypotenuse is equal to the sum of the square on the other two sides. This just means this big, big square here, is equal in area to this little, little one plus this middle, middle one... "

She had drawn a large right-angled triangle and had sketched squares on each of the three sides. It was clear enough to Tanker that the square on the big side was about the size of the two smaller squares put together.

"I can see that, Lu. I mean it's bloody obvious. But I can't very well write that in the exam can I? I can't write, 'It is true because you can bloody well see it's true!'!"

"Listen and learn, Tommy!"

She was at it again, calling him Tommy. But Tanker hadn't time to argue with her. The exams were only around the corner and he felt sure that if he could pick up on this geometery he would at least get a pass in maths. He sipped the tea as she explained slowly and clearly how to prove that something that was obvious to the naked eye could also be shown mathematically.

Once he had grasped how to prove the theorem he set about doing it on his own. Lucy was quite pleased with herself. Tanker seemed to pick up on her instruction easily.

"Will you show me the rest?"

"Tanker! It would take weeks to cover all the things you don't know!"

"Just a couple then?"

"Okay. It's revision for myself anyway."

As he listened to Lucy things seemed so simple. Problems he had considered beyond him suddenly were no longer problems. He could solve them. He marvelled at the way Lucy tackled each one. How she pointed to the page then to a blank sheet where Tanker found himself getting to the solution in logical steps. Alternate angles were equal and he knew why. Algebraic fractions, integers, venn diagrams, quadratic equations... things he never understood before suddenly became less cloudy, as Lucy took away the mystery.

For the first time in their lifetime of knowing each other Tanker felt differently towards Lucy. She rolled her nose-ring and smiled as he solved each problem. A certain warm feeling arose between them as if they were at the beginning of something. Tanker didn't know what it was, but he liked it.

Chapter 9

Kick the Can

"I knew it all the time that there was drugs going on in that school!"

"They didn't find anything, Dad!"

"That means nothing. The guards were there. That means they know. Just because they didn't find anything doesn't mean that there are no drugs."

Tanker's dad hated drugs more than anything else in life. It was his favourite topic of conversation.

"I'll tell you one thing, Tanker boy, keep away from that scene!"

Tanker laughed.

"Me! How in the name of God could I get involved in all that?"

"I've seen it inside, Tanker. Decent fellows like yourself from decent homes. They start off like yourself saying, 'No way, not me!' Then before they know it they're in!"

"I don't think you'll have to worry about me, Dad."

Tanker meant what he was saying. He had heard of kids at school going on about smoking pot and getting E and stuff but he had never actually seen anybody at it. He had seen cider parties at the back of the estate up on the embankment but he never saw any drugs. As far as Tanker was concerned the drugs thing was a lot of hot air. Kids trying to sound tough.

When he had arrived back from Lucy's flat he felt elated. He now knew that he would not fail maths. At least he wouldn't fail by much. Dad had cooked a big stew for the dinner which Tanker served up for the two of them. His mother worked as a cleaner in the local branch of Allied Irish

Banks. She wouldn't be in until after seven. Even though she was still finding it difficult to get used to having her husband back at home, it was pleasant for both herself and Tanker having somebody to cook the dinner.

"There isn't a lot of meat but I used a ton of vegetables and there's loads of spuds!"

"That's great, Dad. I was thinking of going vegetarian anyway!"

"You? Vegetarian?"

"Why not?"

"Come off it! You couldn't live without meat!"

"I could."

"Fine! You can start now! Give me your plate! I'll take your meat and you can have some of my parsnips."

"Wow! Not so fast, Dad! I was only thinking about it!" Tanker meant what he was saying. Lucy was certainly getting through to him.

Yeoman was gone when Tanker called. Celia opened the door in her nurse's uniform. Tanker's mouth went dry. As usual. He anticipated another teasing session. It didn't come. The usually funny and bubbly Celia was on this occasion somewhat subdued.

"He's not here. Bye, Tanker," she said as she closed the door abruptly.

This wasn't like Celia. She normally kept him there for ages smiling and flirting with him. Maybe she had things on her mind. Boyfriend trouble or something. He was sure it wasn't anything personal but nonetheless he was surprised.

As Tanker made his way to the stairs he heard shouting coming from the Dunne's flat. It sounded like Mr Dunne. Yeoman's father was normally a quiet man. He usually spent his days watching the telly or reading books from the library. Now he was roaring at someone. Tanker couldn't make out what he was saying.

When he arrived at the snooker hall nobody had seen Yeoman. He hadn't been in. Tanker hung around for a while waiting for someone he recognised to ask him to play a frame. He didn't have to wait too long.

"Hey, Tanker, fancy your chances against the shark here?" It was Ponch from the soccer team who had just been wiped out by Pats O'Shaugnessy, the best snooker player on the northside.

"Just my luck!" moaned Tanker. "I probably won't even get to pot a ball!"

Tanker did succeed in potting a ball right from the break. Unfortunately for him it was the white one for which he gave his opponent four free points and the chance to clear the table. Pats was deadly accurate and more or less won the game with a break of fifty. Tanker did manage to pot a few reds but, even with Pats not trying very hard, he was wiped out within twenty minutes.

"Another one?" asked Pats.

"No point, Pats. You'll only hammer me. I think I'll head. You didn't see Yeoman by any chance, did you?"

"No. But it's funny that you ask."

"Why so?"

"There were a couple of heavies in here a while ago looking for him too."

"Heavies? What do you mean?"

"Well not the type of guys you'd like to bump into in a dark alley!"

"What did they want with Yeoman?"

"I don't know. All I told them was I hadn't seen him in weeks. Which is true. He hasn't been here for ages. That's very unlike him. The guy used to live here. He was getting pretty hot as well. Last time I played him he had a break of sixty."

Tanker made his way back to the Mansions. He was worried about Yeoman. Who were these so-called heavies and what did they want with him? What had he been up to?

At the entrance to the Mansions he noticed a can of coke perched on a low wall. He wouldn't have given it a second glance only that he noticed the ring-pull was still attatched. It was one of those special Superball cans.

He picked up the can and was surprised to discover that it was still quite full. He snapped off the ring-pull and began to pour the coke onto the grass behind the wall. He was just about to drop kick the can into the car-park when he felt the blow to his head.

"Leave that can alone, asshole!"

Tanker put his hands up to the back of his head where he felt blood seeping from an open wound. As he looked up he saw the baseball bat coming down. He put his arm up to block the swing and roared in agony as the bat thundered down repeatedly on him.

"Please leave me alone!" he roared between the raining blows. He begged his assailant to stop hitting him. "I didn't know it was your can! I'm sorry!"

The guy with the baseball bat dragged Tanker to his feet. He was wearing a crash helmet with a tinted visor, making it impossible to see his face. Not that Tanker would have been able to see him anyway as his vision was blurred from both the blow to his head and the pain from his shoulder.

"I only wanted the ring-pull! I didn't know it was your coke!"

"Don't come the innocent with me, you stupid thick heap of... !"

"Honestly, sir! Look I'm sorry! Please don't kill me! Let me go! Please!"

"Just don't touch things that don't belong to you!" The words were spat rather than spoken. In order to drive the message home he smashed his helmet-clad head down on Tanker's face before dropping his victim like a sack of potatoes to the ground.

Tanker heard the bike revving up and speeding away. He pulled himself up and staggered into the lift. His shoulder made each movement difficult yet he was so relieved to be still alive he seemed to find an extra degree of strength.

"Tanker! What happened?" Lucy had heard the commotion below and had run down the stairs before Tanker had a chance to press the fourth floor button in the lift.

"I took some guy's can of coke by mistake!"

Chapter 10

The Renault Ladies

Tanker woke up to the sound of breakfast trolleys rattling outside in the corridor. The air was thick with the hospital aroma of disinfectant and tea. He was in a large ward which he seemed to be sharing with several old men all wearing floral-patterned pyjamas. He propped his pillows up behind him and sat up without too much pain.

Apart from feeling stiff and sore he was relieved that his injuries were not too serious. His parents had called late last night but he sent them off telling them that he was fine and that he would probably be home in the morning. He told them nothing about the beating he had received and had warned Lucy to tell them nothing either.

"The line is I tripped on the steps and banged my head on the railings and that you saw it happen!"

"But, Tanker, they deserve to know the truth."

"And what good would that do? They'd only start fussing and insist on collecting me every time I'd go out. No, Lu, the story is I was coming up the steps, you were coming down and I slipped and fell."

Remarkably nobody questioned this version of events. Tanker's mother decided to write to the corporation and complain about the state of the steps in the Mansions.

"You're not the first person to fall on those steps, Tanker. Mrs Murray on the fifth floor broke her wrist last January. On a wet day they're a disgrace. Water everywhere. And that caretaker fella, Benny! Sure that fella is never sober! I'm surprised nobody's ever been killed! I'll give them a piece of my tongue at City Hall, I can tell you!"

"Although it hasn't rained for a week. The steps couldn't

have been wet!" His father was a little more dubious, although he also appeared to accept Tanker's explanation. "Probably fell over your bloody laces. You always were a bit of a bull in a china shop, Tanker."

Tanker didn't like lying to his parents but he felt that, in his own way, he was protecting them. They wouldn't have been able to do anything anyway. They had enough to do getting their marriage back on track without this added worry. Besides, as far as he was concerned, it was over. He got picked on. He got done in. He survived. Case closed.

After a breakfast of soggy cornflakes, damp cold toast and milky tea Celia Dunne popped her head around Tanker's screen and announced that she thought he was being let home.

"I think the doc will be around in about ten minutes to tell you but I've seen the x-rays and you seem to be in one piece. I'll drive you home if you like. I'm coming off duty at eight. Oh, and sorry about being a bit bitchy when you called to our place last night!"

With that she was off again as the doctor entered the ward carrying Tanker's file and reading it as she walked. She was the same doctor who had been on duty when Tanker was admitted the night before. Her badge said her name was Doctor Patricia Conway but she told Tanker to call her Pat. She looked about eighteen but she was obviously more. She reminded Tanker of the lady in this telly-ad for Renault cars but, then again, in Tanker's eyes, so did most eighteen-year-olds.

Tanker strained his eyes to read what was printed under her name. "Senior Registrar". That made her a bit older than eighteen, he guessed, but what the hell. Tanker sat up as she perched on the edge of the bed and smiled.

"Nothing too serious, Thomas. You have a bruised rib on the left-hand side here!"

She felt it as she spoke. Tanker winced in pain but smiled

as if he had felt nothing.

"Your nose isn't broken. The shoulder is fine, just badly bruised. You had some concussion, that's why we kept you in here overnight but I think that's cleared now. So if there are no other problems you can go."

"Great! I'll just get my things from the locker... "

The doctor didn't move from the bed. She continued to look at Tanker as he made his way towards the lockers inside the doors of the ward.

Tanker stopped and returned to the bed.

"Is there something wrong, doctor?"

"You tell me, Thomas."

"How do you mean?"

"Well, you come in here last night with injuries that are consistent with a vicious beating. Then you tell us that you fell."

Tanker blushed. He knew she knew he was lying. He would have loved to confide in her and tell her the truth. Then they could both hop into her Renault and elope to some back of beyond place and live happily ever after. But unfortunately he lived in the real world. He was scared. She would pass on his story to the gardaí. He didn't want the guards involved. He had grown up associating the guards with one thing. Locking up his father. He didn't trust them. He just wanted to get home and forget about what had happened. In future he would just be careful and not pick up anything that didn't belong to him.

"I fell."

"Are you sure?"

"Certain."

She nodded as Tanker had the final word then told him to sign the form she was holding. She told him that he was free to go once his parents came to collect him.

Tanker dressed quickly and made his way out of the ward where Celia was waiting for him.

"No need to wait for your folks, Tanker, I've signed the

discharge form."

Tanker smiled as he sat into the passenger seat of Celia's battered sixteen-year-old Renault.

"What are you laughing at?"

"Nothing!" he said as the engine choked and spluttered its way back to Terence MacSwiney Mansions.

Chapter 11

Truth Hurts

Celia came right out with it. Yeoman was involved in drugs. That was why she had been short with Tanker when he had called to the flat the night before. Apparently her father had just been paid a visit by the guards. The fire drill in the school had given them information.

"But they found nothing. They just came and went." Tanker found this hard to believe.

"That's what they wanted everyone to believe. They called to our place yesterday afternoon looking for Yeoman."

"His jacket!" said Tanker. "They must have found the gear in his jacket."

"So you knew about it too, Tanker!"

"No, Celia, honest. He told me nothing. It's just that we went to Greasies for breakfast and Yeoman never stopped going on about his jacket. He nearly killed poor old Dopey Dick for not letting him back in to the school to get it. Then when he found it afterwards he looked as if he had won the Lotto."

"Well, the guards aren't going to do much. They only found a couple of joints, probably not enough to charge him. They're going to let him off with a warning. But they still want to know who is supplying him. The thing is though, Tanker, we know that Yeoman isn't just a runner. He started off as one but lately he got greedy. He's been selling the stuff too."

"How come?"

"Because there is no way he could afford to buy it."

Tanker didn't have to be told. Running drugs was common in the Mansions. Celia explained it to him even though he had heard it all before. Pushers came into an area and organised runners, like Yeoman, to move the gear for them.

These runners got a small money commission or else they held some dope for themselves. Yeoman had started out as a runner but now, according to Celia, he was taking extra dope and trying to sell it himself.

"The thing is the guards want Yeoman to name names."

"And Yeoman won't!" Tanker knew his friend.

"That's the trouble. He either doesn't know who they are or else he's just too afraid to name them. Maybe you'll be able to find out from him."

"Me?"

"Well, you are his best friend. He tells you everything."

"He didn't tell me about this. This is the first I've heard about it."

"Well, you could ask him, Tanker."

"Yeah, and then what? Tell you, is it? Or do I go straight to the guards and inform on me best mate? Probably end up without me kneecaps into the bargain!"

"That's not what I'm saying. I just thought you might get him to own up to the guards. He's in big trouble, Tanker."

"And you think I should join him? Sorry, Celia, but Yeoman obviously didn't need my advice when he got mixed up in all of this."

"But you will try and talk to him? Please?"

Celia Dunne flashed one of those smiles at Tanker that made him feel weak all over. It was the same feeling he always got every time she opened the door of the flat to him. How could he refuse? He muttered something about not promising anything and she reached over and kissed his cheek. She smelt of disinfectant and hospital but somewhere in between Tanker caught a distinctive waft of her perfume.

"Oh God, Tanker, if you were five years older I'd run away with you!"

I could always pretend, thought Tanker. But he didn't say it. He just blushed.

Chapter 12

The Concerned Parent

Tanker spent the rest of the day lying on the couch watching Eurosport with his father whose suspicions continued to be roused. They were watching some claycourt tennis match between two players with unpronounceable names. Tanker hadn't much interest in the game but it gave him the opportunity not to talk to his father, or at least to deflect his questions with one-word answers. Tom Kelly's intention was to nag his son into submission. Every five minutes he would probe and prod at the sketchy details of Tanker's story until it would begin to fall apart.

"It was a dry night."

"So?"

"So the steps couldn't have been wet. They only get slippy when they are wet."

"Slippery."

"What?"

"You said 'slippy'. No such word. It's slippery!"

"You know what I bloody well mean!"

"Look, Dad, I slipped on the steps and fell. You're right, the steps weren't slippy or slippery. They were bone dry. I tripped up on my shoe lace. Like you said in the hospital, I'm like a bull in a china shop. Be quiet, would you. I'm trying to watch this. The blondie guy is on set point."

"Velcro!"

"Is that his name. I thought it was something 'osky'!"

"You heard me! I said velcro! Your shoes, Tanker!"

"What?"

"Your runners don't have laces. They have velcro!"

"Damn, Osky missed it."

Tanker pretended not to have heard and continued to

stare at the tennis while he thought of a way of worming his way out of the hole in which he had buried himself.

"Deuce again. This is some match!"

"Tanker, velcro. You don't have laces in your runners!"

"Hmm... Oh yeah... Well you know what I mean... I just tripped. Clumsy old me! Two left feet and all that! Okay, now just leave it, will you?"

"Tell me the truth, Tanker. What happened?"

"Why the inquisition?"

"Because I know a liar when I hear one. When it comes to telling lies and falsifying events I'm your man!"

"Years of practice, I suppose!"

"Something like that. Lying to Detective Inspectors and High Court judges carries a very high skill factor. A skill that you obviously haven't got."

"I'm not lying. I slipped and fell. Now would you ever go away and leave me alone. Wow! Great shot! Advantage Blondie!"

Tom Kelly Senior stood up and announced that he was going to make tea. His son accepted the offer of a cup and hoped that this would be the end of all the questions. Some hope!

"There's one lesson in the lying game that you have to be very careful of, son."

"What's that, Dad?"

"Never trust anybody with the truth!"

"Lucy!" whispered Tanker.

"Game set and match to your old man!"

His father nodded more in relief than triumph as he made his way to the kitchen and put on the kettle.

"She told me about the guy on the motorbike."

Tanker's immediate response was to go around to Lucy and do some head-butting of his own. He was gripped by a desire to pull out her nose-rings. However, he was somewhat relieved that the lying was over.

Tom Kelly made the tea and brought it in to Tanker. The two sat and stared as Blondie with the unpronounceable name which ended in "osky" took the first set.

"What did you think I was going to do, Tanker? Go after every biker in Cork and beat the crap out of them?"

Tanker grinned at the thought.

"I wouldn't put it past you."

"There's nothing that can be done. Except to tell you to keep your eyes open in future. It might be an idea to let your mam or I know what time you'll... "

"Dad!" Tanker was firm. This was the very reason for not telling. He was nearly fifteen years old. He didn't need kid glove treatment.

"Okay, but your mother would be really pissed off if she know you had lied to her. She has a letter written to the Lord Mayor demanding that he come around and inspect the steps up to the balconies here. She wants a full-time caretaker to replace that drunken idiot Benny."

Benny was a part-time caretaker whose claim to fame was his inability to take care of himself, let alone a block of flats. He spent most of his days drinking cider and sleeping on a bench in the courtyard in front of the flats.

"Well that wouldn't do any harm, would it?"

"Except it wouldn't be the truth. Benny had nothing to do with your 'fall', did he?"

Tanker got up. He had had enough of this fatherly concern for one afternoon. While he felt guilty in one sense for not telling his father the truth there was also a nagging sense of "who the hell does he think he is?" Formerly the Jack The Lad of petty crime... now The Concerned Parent. How many times in the past had he been banged up when Tanker needed him? First Holy Communion Day, first match for Rovers, first match for the school team, parent-teacher meetings, the school play when he had the lead role of Aladdin, the time he played Joseph in the Christmas pageant? Where was his father then? In a eight by ten cell, that's where! Who in the name of God did he think he was now? Drink your tea, Dad thought Tanker angrily as he put on his jacket.

"I just think you should show a little more consideration... for your mother. You must tell us what's happening, what's going on. I think it would be a good idea in the future if... "

Tanker had heard enough.

"I don't care what you bloody well think! You breeze back here for five minutes and suddenly you're Superdad! Well you're not! And you never were! Do you want to know what I used to tell kids in primary school when they asked me about my dad? I told them he was dead! I told them I didn't have one!"

His father stood there. Stung. Hurt washed through him ridding him of any other feelings. He didn't reply. He just watched his son as he made his way to the door.

"Where are you going?" he asked, somewhat inevitably.

"Out!"

Chapter 13

Not Just Any Old Can

Yeoman was coming down the steps from his flat en route to Tanker just as Tanker rounded the corner of the fourth floor landing. Like his friend, Yeoman had been suffering from an overdose of fatherly advice only his was far more threatening. More along the lines of "get your act together fast or I'll break your head". Like Tanker, Yeoman too, was unable to hold his tongue. He told his father that if he hadn't been so bloody idle then he wouldn't have to sell a bit of dope to make a few pounds.

Ever since he had been laid off from the dockyard all Eddie Dunne ever did was watch endless videos and place imaginary bets on horses he couldn't afford to back. And now he was telling his son that making money was wrong.

"It's not the money! It's how you're making the money! Selling those E things and that dope stuff!"

"It's harmless, Dad! All the kids are doing it!"

"Drugs kill son!"

"That's a load of crap, Dad! E is just a bit of fun and all dope does is make you laugh!"

"What a stupid thing to say!"

"It's true. Dope makes you want to laugh. Where's the harm in that? You should try it some time! When was the last time you had a good laugh?"

"It's wrong, Yeoman!" Eddie Dunne was screeching. "And if you keep this up you'll end up spending your life banged up!"

"And what's the alternative, Dad? End up like you is it! Organising fantasy horse racing leagues and looking forward to the hourly cup of tea? Get real!"

Eddie Dunne could take no more of this. He stood up aggressively as if he was going to hit him. However, Veronica

Dunne got there first and planted a firm slap on the face of her son. Veronica always seemed to find herself in that position. In the middle. The peacemaker. Only this time she sided firmly with her husband. How dare he speak to her husband like that.

"Get out, you little pup, and don't come back until you're man enough to apologise to your father!"

"I'm sorry!" Yeoman heard himself say almost by reflex as he felt his stinging cheek and the loud buzzing of the clatter rang in his ear.

His father returned to his armchair and turned the volume up. It was the same tennis match that the Kelly father and son had been watching. He had placed an imaginary hundred pounds on the blond guy to win in straight sets. Suddenly he felt very lonely.

Yeoman was feeling a mixture of self-pity and guilt. He nodded to Tanker by way of saying hello. Tanker nodded back and the two headed down the steps and out through the car-park in robot-like fashion. They didn't speak. Tanker was waiting for Yeoman to bring the subject up. Yeoman was letting his mind simmer down first.

They went into the park and sat on two swings. Apart from a mother watching her twin toddlers go up and down the slide there was nobody else around.

"Sorry about what happened."

Tanker nodded.

"That's okay, Yeoman. Not your fault."

"I think it might have been."

"How come?"

Yeoman didn't just think that Tanker's beating might have beeen his fault, he was one hundred per cent certain.

"That can you picked up. Did you see inside it?"

"Inside it? No. It was full of coke. I just wanted the ring pull. I promised Dunnzer I'd give him my extras for the Superball."

Yeoman was filling up with guilt. It was bad enough that his friend got beaten up due to his mistake. It was even worse to discover that he was only doing his kid brother a favour.

"It's this running thing I was doing."

"Yeah?"

"I was to leave the can inside the bin but the bin was too empty. I was afraid that the stuff would fall out if I let it fall to the end so I left it balancing on the top."

"What stuff?" Tanker had an idea but he was playing dumb.

"It was just some dope wrapped up in tin foil and insulating tape. There might have been some E as well. I don't know. I was just told where to pick it up and where to leave it down."

"So you're running stuff and you don't even know what kind of stuff it is?"

"You don't ask questions in this game. It's just running. Pick it up. Leave it down. Cans. Bottles. You just follow orders. Ask no questions."

"You're crazy, Yeoman. There could have been anything in that package. Heroin, crack... "

"Don't be daft!"

"I'm not daft!"

Yeoman didn't respond. He got off the swing and lit a cigarette, pretending to stare at something in the distance as he blew the smoke idly out of the side of his mouth. He turned and faced Tanker again. It was time to talk.

He had messed everything up. It had all sounded so simple at the outset. All he had to do was run the stuff. Collect it at point A, deliver it to point B. Two quid a run. Three runs a night, sometimes four. But then he got greedy. Started looking for dope of his own to sell on the side. He wanted to make some real money. Sell directly to the client. Ready-made joints. E on demand. He was in the ideal position to set it up. There was a ready-made market at St Peters. A simple strategy of supply and demand. Nothing could have been simpler. At least not until that Dopey Dick got in the way and wouldn't let him in to get his jacket.

"For God's sake, Yeoman, you're crazy!"

"I'm even crazier than you think, Tanker."

"How come?"

"I made a mess of that run when you got the hiding. They won't let me run any more. The guy on the bike is called The Biker. He works in a team overseeing all operations. Anyone who screws up is out. I screwed up."

"So the Biker reported you?"

"Yeah. I'm out. And the problem is I'm in big trouble."

"I got some dope to sell in school. I thought I'd go it alone. The Biker organised it with his boss."

"Who is he?"

"Not a he. A she. It's a woman. The Queen."

"The Queen. Wasn't she the one on the telly? That *Prime Time* thing last year. The one about drugs in Cork. She was the one the guards would love to lock up but she always gets away. They call her the Untouchable."

"Yep! That's the Queen!"

"What's her real name."

"I don't know. No names."

"Don't tell me, she lives in the Palace!"

"I don't know where she lives. I've never met her. That's how it works. No names. No information. That's the way it works. That's why she's escaped jail so far. She delegates everything to her pushers. I've never seen any of them, apart from the Biker and he always has that helmet covering his face. I wouldn't recognise him if I met him without it. Anyway, I'm owed two hundred quid from different kids in school to pay her back. But they won't pay up. They certainly won't pay up now that they know I'm out of it."

"Why not?"

Yeoman stared at his friend with that "don't-you-understand-anything?" look. Tanker suddenly realised why.

"Of course. You're out now. You won't be getting any more stuff to supply them so why should they pay you what they owe?"

"Something like that. You can be sure that already somebody has taken my place with the running."

"And what happens if you don't come up with the two hundred quid?"

Yeoman sighed. The answer was obvious. If Tanker was nearly murdered by the Biker for inadvertently picking up the wrong can what would happen to a pusher who didn't pay his dues?

The two friends sat in silence as if each was waiting for the other to offer some magical solution. Tanker would have loved more than anything to be able to say, "No problem, I'll sort it!" but it wasn't that type of situation. This was no superhero scenario. It was a huge mess. Yeoman had succeeded in digging himself into a hole from which there was no escape.

"I don't have two hundred but I can give you ten a week if I work an extra night in Joe's!"

"I couldn't expect you to do that, Tanker. That's your money. You need it."

"Look, Yeoman. You're in deep trouble here. This is the best I can do so don't come over all oh-no-I-couldn't with me. I'm not some stranger. It's me! Tanker! Blood Brother. Or don't you remember?"

Yeoman sighed as if he hadn't thought about that in a long time.

"Yeah, of course I remember. I still have the piece of paper, actually."

Tanker was pleased to hear that.

"But I couldn't take the money from you, Tanker. Besides, the Queen probably wouldn't agree to a tenner a week."

"Well why don't we go and ask Joe to take you on as well.

He's always going on about being stuck for staff. If you worked each night of the weekend plus weekday nights during the holidays you'll surely be able to pay off this Queen person."

Tanker watched as Yeoman's face began to brighten.

"Why don't we go and see him now? I'll tell him that we can share my nights and that you'll do any extra work on top of that!"

"That sounds fine, Tanker, but are you sure? I mean it would be your nights I'd be taking from you."

"No sweat! Anyway me mam hates me working there! Come on, lets go and see Joe."

Tanker wasn't entirely convinced that Joe liked Yeoman but he was determined to talk him into it. As they walked out into Green Street he was mentally putting together his please-give-Yeoman-a-break speech.

"He's dead sound, Joe. He won't leave you down. I'll train him in for you myself. It won't cost you a penny. Give him a trial. You'll see. He's as honest as the day is long! Very quiet. Never in any hassle." Some of this was going to have to be delivered with a stiff straight face.

As they came to the top of Green Street and headed into Blackpool, Tanker realised that his speech would not now be necessary. Yeoman stood as if he had been frozen to the spot!

"Jesus, Tanker, look at that!"

"Oh my God! I don't believe it!"

They stood wide-eyed as the flames from Joe's Diner leapt ferociously into the night air.

Chapter 14

Joe

Nothing prepared Tanker for the shock he experienced the night Joe's Diner burned down. He watched the terrifying scene from behind a police barricade across the road. Two fire-brigades were fighting the blaze. A crowd of onlookers had gathered. Most of them were as dumbstruck as Tanker, silently staring through the black smoke cloud which had filled the street at the flames lashed out angrily.

A gang of airheads were among them as well. Swigging from cider bottles they cheered every crash of broken glass and each flame which had outjumped the rest.

"Two chicken suppers, Joe, when you get a chance!"

"The curry sauce is very hot tonight, Joe!"

"Joe! I'll have my burger well done!"

"I want mine flame-grilled!"

Each smart comment was greeted with a chorus of approving laughter. Tanker was raging. He would have loved to have rammed a fist down one of their jeering throats but decided that it was neither the right time nor place. Yeoman stood open-mouthed, shaking his head in disbelief.

"This cannot be happening, Tanker! It's just unbelievable!"

"I wonder is Joe okay? And Phil! Jesus! Phil! She might have been upstairs lying down! Did she get out?"

"Why don't you ask someone? That guard might know."

Tanker leapt over the barricade and made his way towards the guard who had already spotted him and came charging in his direction.

"You idiot! Get back behind that barrier! We've got enough to be getting on with without any hassle from the likes of you and that mob of yours!"

The likes of me? Great, thought Tanker. A guard with an

attitude problem. A tar-them-all-with-the-same-brush attitude, but this was no time to take offence.

"It's okay, guard. I work there. Part-time. I'm a friend of the owner Joe. I just want to tell you that I think his wife might be upstairs in bed. She has a bad back. Disc trouble... "

Tanker didn't get a chance to finish his sentence. The explosion rocked the entire street, sending shards of broken glass flying in all directions. By reflex Tanker flung himself at the guard and they both lay huddled in the middle of the street as the window pane fragments and debris showered them. There was a long silence which was followed by screaming. Tanker was half-afraid to move in case any bodily movement from him might trigger another bang.

"Are you okay, son?" The voice came from underneath him.

"I think so. Something hit me on the head but it wasn't that heavy. Just a bit of a bump, that's all."

"Good lad. Er, you might move now so I can get up."

Tanker rolled onto his side, allowing the garda to stand up.

"Thanks son. That was quick thinking of you. I won't forget it in a hurry. What's your name?"

"Thomas Kelly, but they call me Tanker."

"Good man, Thomas. I'll see you later. Now I better get back to work."

Tanker sat on the kerb behind the barricade and watched the garda return to join in the mayhem. There were uniforms everywhere. Nurses, doctors, paramedics, firefighters, police and members of Civil Defence seemed to suddenly appear as if by magic. Maybe it was the bang on the head he had received, but Tanker didn't remember their arriving.

Sirens and blue flashing lights, screams and bloodied bandaged heads gave the whole street an unreal sense of light and sound. Ambulance personnel were giving on the spot first aid, dressing head wounds and telling people to relax and that everything would be fine. More spectators flocked to the scene. The gardaí were appealing to them to stay behind the barriers. Tanker heard one guard telling people over and over again that nobody had been killed. It was a large gas bottle that had exploded and all injuries were minor. Everything was being taken care of.

The fire blazed even higher as more brigades screeched into the street. Sirens continued to blare. Blue lights continued to flash. Someone somewhere was yelling hysterically into a loudhaler, telling everybody to stay calm, that the emergency services would very soon bring the fire under control.

It's a pity someone can't bring you under control, thought Tanker.

"You okay, Tanker?" It was Yeoman. Tanker looked up from the kerb and nodded.

"Just the back of my head. Something fell on me while I was lying down."

"Does it hurt?"

"Not really. It's just throbbing a bit."

Tanker slowly raised himself, brushing tiny pieces of glass and dust from his head and shoulders in the process. He rubbed the bump which was beginning to rise to the size of a ping-pong ball.

"I wonder what hit me?" he muttered.

"This I think." Yeoman reached down and picked it up. It was a large plastic sign dangling from its splintered wooden frame. Tanker read the two words. A lump rose in his throat. JOE'S DINER.

"Do you think he's okay, Yeoman?"

Tanker longed for his friend to say "yes" but he didn't. Yeoman shrugged his shoulders and looked away. Tanker knew he didn't want to make eye contact. That would have been a give-away. Yeoman's eyes would have spelt out the one word Tanker didn't want to hear. They would have said "no".

At midnight they found Joe's body. The garda upon whom

Tanker had thrown himself came and told them.

"Sorry, son. I think we found your friend. His wife wasn't in the building. Apparently she had gone around to her parents' house for the evening. Awful business."

Tanker sat stunned. Yeoman pulled him to his feet.

"Come on, Tank, let's go. There's no point in staying any longer."

"Your friend is right, Thomas. You head off home. I'm Sergeant Ted Donnelly. I'll call and see you tomorrow. Do you live nearby?"

Tanker stared into space. He had heard the question. In fact he had heard everything the garda had said to him. He had heard Yeoman answering for him. The flats. Terence. MacSwiney. Mansions. Fourth. Floor. Number. Forty. Four. Okay. Son. See. You. Tomorrow. Bye. For. Now. It was if he was being spoken to through a long tunnel and he was unable to speak back. Besides there was nothing to say. Joe was dead. His friend Joe was dead. There was nothing to say.

Chapter 15

Messenger Boy

A week after Joe's funeral Tanker was still confused as to why it had happened. The papers all said it was an accident. That was the official garda line. An accident. He knew it could never have been.

Joe was meticulous about his chipper. The best chipper in Ireland was his boast and he worked sixteen hours a day to make sure that his customers agreed.

Nothing went unchecked. Safety and hygiene seemed to be Joe's twin obsessions. All plugs were disconnected at closing time. He had a fire alarm both upstairs and down and fire blankets and extinquishers in every corner. The friers were serviced twice a year and replaced whenever newer models came on the market. He used top quality vegetable oil which he changed daily before scrubbing the inside of each frier with water close to boiling point. Joe's chipper was his palace and there was no way he would ever leave room for an accident.

The funeral was private. Immediate family only. Tanker thought about going as he had always felt part of Joe's family. However, when the morning of the funeral arrived he simply couldn't face it. He decided he would visit Phil the following week. She was staying with her parents in Douglas. That's where she had been the night of the fire. Sergeant Donnelly told him that when he visited the day before the funeral.

As it turned out Sergeant Donnelly knew Tom Kelly Senior very well. He had arrested him on numerous occasions in the past. However, when they met in the flat that morning they were like old school-friends who hadn't met for years.

"You've a great lad there, Tom! He saved my bacon the

other night, I can tell you!"

"Ah, he's a chip of the old block, Sergeant!" Tom Kelly joked.

"He takes after his mother, Sergeant!" Ann Kelly chipped in. Tanker was beginning to squirm with embarrassment.

"I'll promise you one thing, Sergeant Donnelly. I'll not be going back inside. I've seen the light. I've too much to lose on the outside."

"I'm glad to hear it, Tom."

"If I could only get a nice little job for myself I'd be the happiest man in Cork. That's the trouble though. Who'd give a job to an ex-con? I mean to say... "

Sergeant Donnelly smiled and sipped his tea. Tanker watched him sitting there listening politely as his father rambled on. He wished to hell he'd shut up. He was embarrassing him. Donnelly had probably heard ex-prisoners talking like this numerous times in the past. Another case of the same old story.

The following Friday morning Tanker was sitting at the window of the flat. His father was in the kitchen wearing his wife's apron. He was making dinner with the radio turned up full belt. They hadn't spoken about the row they had had. Any time Tanker had tried to bring it up his father had deflected him. It was as if he knew it was coming and he didn't want to hear it. He kept being cheerful all the time, never missing the opportunity to crack a joke.

"Did you hear that, Tanker? On the Gay Byrne Show! There's a guy after robbing the AIB in Wilton dressed as a nun. He got away with sixty grand. Just strolled up to the counter and handed the cashier a note saying 'Sixty grand or start saying your prayers, sister'." Jesus, what's the world coming to! Your man Gaybo is talking to the manager. Can you hear it there?"

Tanker had to shout to try and make himself heard above

the crackling voice of Gay Byrne on the radio.

"The whole of Cork can hear it, Dad. If you turn it up any louder the whole of Dublin will hear it too."

"What was that?"

"Nothing, Dad!"

"Will I mash the spuds or do you want them whole?"

"Mash."

"What?"

"Mash them!"

Down in the car-park Dunnzer was organising yet another replay of the Cup Final telling all that this was going to be a cliffhanger with both teams anxious for glory at the end of a difficult season.

"Dunnzer, throw down the can and shut up!"

"Yeah, Dunnzer, get on with it!"

Seconds later the sound of the can scraping on the tarmacadamed yard grated Tanker's ears. He went to look for his football to throw down to them. As he rummaged through the bottom of the hot press, the doorbell rang.

"If that's the guards, tell them I didn't do it. I'm innocent. Anyway I'm not in the habit of dressing as a nun! Hah! Do you get it, Tank? Habit? Nun? Hah hah!"

"Hilarious, Dad, next stop 'The Stand-Up Show'!"

Tanker jumped back when he opened the door. Christ! A ghost! For a split second he thought he was looking at Joe. The same round face and dark features. The same height, even though Joe was slightly heavier.

"Hello, are you Tanker?"

"Yeah... er, who are you?"

"I'm Sean Brady, Joe's brother, may I come in?"

"Oh... of course, yes. Er, would you like a cup of tea, Mr Brady?"

"Please call me Sean. And yes, I'd love a cup."

"Come on into the kitchen. Dad, this is Joe's brother, Sean. Sean this is Tom, my dad."

Tom Kelly wiped his greasy fingers on his wife's apron before shaking Sean Brady's extended hand.

"How do you do, Sean? Er... I was so sorry to hear about Joe... we all were... it was an awful thing to happen. He was a great fellow. Very good to our Tanker here. Very good."

"Thanks, Tom. Joe spoke very well of you too, Tanker. He always said how he would have been lost without you."

"Do you know what I can't understand, Sean, is how it happened. I mean to say, Tanker there would tell you Joe was always so careful."

Sean shook his head and muttered something about not being able to make it out either. Tanker felt Sean was being evasive. He had a feeling that Sean knew something. Something that might explain the real reason for the fire.

They sat at the kitchen table. Sean did most of the talking. He told them that Phil was at her parents' house the night of the fire. Joe had been killed trying to remove some large gas bottles from the yard at the back of the chipper. That would have accounted for the explosion.

"Anyway, Tanker, I have a photography and printing business in Oliver Plunkett Street. I do lots of desktop publishing work, personalised stationery, posters, fliers and that sort of thing. The thing is Róisín, my assistant, isn't too happy about working weekends so I was wondering would you be interested? I know Joe would have liked me to offer you the job so if you're interested in doing some courier work on Saturdays and maybe one or two evenings after school... ?"

"You mean delivering stuff?"

"Yes and some work in the office, checking photographs against the negatives, putting them into the jacket envelopes, taking phone calls, making the tea!"

"Great! Thanks, Sean."

"In my day it was called messenger boy! Now it's courier! That's progress for you!" Tom Kelly laughed as he filled up each cup from the steaming pot.

Suddenly Tanker thought of Yeoman. While he was in need of extra cash himself he knew that Yeoman needed it even more.

"Er, there's this friend of mine, Sean. He's called Yeoman. Could I share the job with him? We could take it in turns."

Sean looked at Tanker then at his father who nodded back at him. It was a nod which Sean interpreted as Yeoman's-a-good-lad-too.

"That sounds okay. Here's my card. If you call in to me on Saturday at around eleven I'll show you the ropes. Bring this Yeoman along. I don't have enough work at the moment for the two of you but if you're willing to share the job and the few pounds, then that's up to you. I have bit of a backlog to get through at the moment because I was away on holidays the week before the fire and Róisín came down with a flu and had to close the shop for a few days. I still haven't got around to catching up. You and your friend might be able to help me there."

Tanker grinned with satisfaction. He liked Sean. He was so like Joe it was uncanny. Tanker walked with him down to his car. He was going to the snooker hall anyway to find Yeoman and tell him the good news. Just before he drove away Sean rolled down the window and called to him.

"Tanker, did Joe ever mention anything to you about owing money to anyone?"

Tanker shook his head. Owing money? Joe? No way!

"No. Why would he owe money? The chipper was doing very well. It was packed every night."

"I know but... " Sean sighed as if he was reluctant to say any more. Maybe it was better leaving things unsaid. Tanker wanted to know.

"What is it, Sean?"

"It's just a bit weird. Joe phoned me the day before the fire. He sounded worried. It was the first time I ever heard him saying he was thinking of selling up. He said there were a few bad things happening. A few heavies had called in to the chipper demanding money. Extortion money. When I asked him what he meant he wouldn't say."

"Extortion money?" Tanker had never heard Joe mention anything about that before. "Is that when you have to pay money to people to keep an eye on your property or else... "

" ...they arrange things. A beating or in Joe's case a burning out."

"So that's what you think happened to Joe?"

"Maybe. I don't know... One last thing, Tanker. Did Joe ever mention a person called the Queen?"

Tanker swallowed hard and shook his head. "No, he er... no."

Sean sighed and turned the key in the ignition.

"I'll see you on Saturday, Tanker. Thanks."

"Yeah. Thank you, Sean!"

Tanker made his way across to the snooker hall hoping that Sean hadn't noticed his legs trembling. The Queen. Again! Just who exactly was she?

Chapter 16

Love Hurts

Lucy was going out and really didn't want to talk. She wasn't saying where she was going or with whom and her secrecy was driving Tanker nuts. It was obvious that she was trying to create a good impression as she piled on the make-up and implanted her favourite nose-rings. Tanker wanted to talk about Yeoman and Sean and Joe and the Queen and generally open up and bare his soul to Lucy. Up until now he had been under the impression that Lucy was always there for him. That she was only waiting for the right moment and the two of them would click. The sisterly feeling he had with her all these years had changed. It had, he thought, given way to a new feeling. As Lucy explained theorems and trigonometry to him he had felt a warmth between them. Part of him wanted to hold her. To put his arms around her and feel her closeness. To inhale her fragrance. To kiss her. Properly.

"So you're not going to tell me who he is?"

"Who who is?"

"Don't be smart, Lu, it's obvious you're meeting some guy."

"Maybe it's not a guy!"

"Who is it?"

"It? We've moved on to an 'it' now, have we? That should be interesting. Lucy has a big date with her 'it'!"

Tanker tried to suppress the jealousy which was beginning to well up inside him. It was the one time when he would have loved to have sounded indifferent. Lucy had a date. So what. Big deal. No sweat. Have a nice time, Lu! However, hard as he might try, he could not conceal the fact that the thought annoyed him. He was jealous.

"So you won't tell me who he is?"

"Nope!"

"Why not?"

"Because, Tanker, my sweet lunar twin, I sense the big green monster in your psyche."

"A what in my what?"

"And anyway I don't think you would approve. He's not your type."

"So it is a he!"

"Yep!"

"See you, Lucy!"

"Ah Tanker, don't be like that! I'm only teasing... "

Tanker didn't stay to listen to any more. Lucy might have told him more but he didn't want to hear. How could she do this to him? Just as things were going well between them she finds somebody else. Just as things were moving in a new exciting direction she had to spoil it all.

For Tanker, Lucy was becoming less of a girl friend, and more of a girlfriend. As in real girlfriend. She was changing and he liked the changes. He had hoped that she had seen the changes in him. He had a few white hairs on his upper lip now. In the sunlight they glistened. It wasn't quite what you would call a moustache but he was getting there. Yeoman told him that if he shaved it would grow back thicker and darker but he was afraid to try that in case it would take too long to reappear. Then Lucy mightn't notice it at all. As he left her flat he slammed the door and immediately made plans to shave. It wouldn't make any difference now.

In his bedroom he lay on the bed and listened to Pink Floyd's *Delicate Sound Of Thunder*. Tanker loved Pink Floyd. Pink Floyd and REM were his favourite bands. They were his only bands. It was a double cassette compilation. He played the track *Shine on You Crazy Diamond*. He listened to the words and thought of Lucy. A crazy diamond. How appropriate.

He jumped off the bed and threw in an REM tape. It was *Automatic for the People*. The first track he heard was

Everybody Hurts. He turned the volume up and sang along.

It wasn't long before his mother came into the bedroom.

"We're trying to watch *Coronation Street!* Turn that rubbish down!"

"It's not rubbish!"

"Okay! It's not rubbish! It's crap! Now turn it down! Now!"

She slammed the door as she left. Tanker got up and turned off the stereo. He walked over to the window. He looked out as a motorbike screeched to a halt below. At first he thought it was the guy who beat him up the night he picked up the wrong can. Then he looked more closely. It wasn't the Biker. It was Leather Jacket.

"I don't believe it!" He shook his head in disbelief as he spoke to the pane, "Slimeball! Lucy's date! How could she?"

He watched as Denis Cummins took off his helmet and shook his hair so that his pony-tail fell into place. He put his helmet under his arm then headed towards the steps. Tanker stood at the window and waited. A few minutes later his suspicions were confirmed. Lucy sat up on to the back of the motorbike as Leather Jacket revved up and headed out into the sunset. The cool clean hero strikes again.

Tanker opened his wardrobe and stared at his reflection in the mirror on the inside of the door. Yes, he was fat. Yes, he was spotty. Yes, he was on the short side. But he was not a slimeball! How could she do this to him?

He waited by the window all night for them to come back. Every now and then he would turn the stereo on but this time with the volume down low so as not to disturb his parents. He heard the low buzzing sound of their conversation and enjoyed the long silences when they were both watching the television.

At ten o'clock his mother brought him in a cup of tea and some cream crackers. She had asked him to come and join them inside the living-room but he lied about having to read a history chapter for the morning. In one sense it wasn't a lie.

He did have a history chapter to read for the morning. However, he had no intention of reading it.

At eleven the motorbike returned. Not all the lights in the car-park were working so it was difficult to see. He could just about make out the outline of Leather Jacket and Lucy. He turned the light off in his own room. He thought this might help him see better. By the time he returned to the window, Denis had already sped away on the bike and Lucy was on her way up the steps to her flat. Tanker felt relieved. At least she was home. At least he was going home. He lay on the bed and listened to her footsteps on the landing outside. He heard her turn the key and close the door behind her. He could go to sleep now.

Chapter 17

The Truth About Denis

Yeoman was waiting for him when he came out of the flat. Tanker was almost finished reading the history chapter he should have read the night before.

"Will I give Lucy a bell?"

"If you like." Tanker tried to sound cool but Yeoman knew from his tone that there was something up.

"What's up with you?"

"Nothing. Come on, it's late."

Lucy appeared at the door just as Yeoman was about to ring the bell.

"History first, then English! Don't you just love Mondays!" Her face was beaming. Tanker was pleased that she wasn't annoyed about his childishness the night before. He had fought with his jealousy all night. By morning he was determined not to let things get any worse. He had decided to try his no-sweat-everything-is-cool approach. It wouldn't be easy but it was his best shot.

"So did you have a nice time last night? ... With Denis?"

"Quite nice, thank you. I'm glad you remembered his real name. The last time you mentioned him I think you used every insult under the sun."

"No I didn't. I just called him Leather Jacket." Tanker tried his best at self-defence.

Yeoman laughed. "Yeah, right! That's when you ran out of names like ponce, poxface and what was that other one... "

"Super Sleazeball." Lucy smiled as she completed the list.

"Okay, okay. I was wrong. I shouldn't have been so hard on him. If he's a friend of yours, Lucy, then that's good enough for me. I'm cool about it. Okay. It's cool."

"Ah Tommy, that's very good of you. Do you really mean that?"

"Yeah... Sure... I mean... no."

"You rat!" Lucy laughed as she pretended to hit him on the head with her history book.

School presented its usual share of headaches for Tanker. He had missed most of the previous week because of the fire. He claimed to be suffering concussion due to the blow to his head. Now, however, he was struggling to catch up. Once again Miss Dawson and maths had him baffled. He sat through her co-ordinate geometery class feeling as if he had been caught in a time warp, where everyone else had travelled years ahead and he had been transported back to the last century.

"Jesus, Lucy, beam me up. What in the name of God is she talking about?" he whispered as Miss Dawson scribbled on the board.

"It's a doddle, Tank, I'll show you tonight."

Tanker felt better when he heard that. At least being a birdbrain at maths would be useful for something.

When he called Lucy ushered him into her kitchen. She had her book ready to explain it all to him. She took about two minutes. Tanker sat in awe. How come he could follow Lucy and yet in Miss Dawson's class he felt like he belonged to another planet? A planet where co-ordinate geometery, distance and slope formulae were alien concepts.

"Therefore it's basically just a map and the coordinates x y tell you where you are on the map."

"That's all?" Tanker was waiting for the catch. There always seemed to be a catch in maths. He always seemed to understand up to a point then wham! He would lose it!

"No catch. There it is, pure and simple. We're on step one. We've only about five more to go. But they don't get too difficult, I promise. Now do section A and I'll see if you're right!"

"Lucy, you're a genius!"

"Of course I am. In a previous existence I invented the wheel! Now, come on, let's see if you've really picked it up!"

He had. He finished the last problem and handed his notebook to her. He knew he had it right. That for Tanker was the funny thing about maths. It was all so easy when you knew how. The hard thing was getting to know how to know how.

Lucy smiled as she read through his work. She nodded and handed it back to him. They spent the next hour working like that. Lucy explaining, Tanker learning, one step at a time.

"Great! You were right! I am a genius!" Lucy closed the book. "Coffee?"

"Only if it's Nicaraguan."

"Good lad. You're learning."

They sat in the kitchen and he watched her make the coffee. She was rattling on about how multi-national coffee giants were putting the smaller coffee nations out of business. Tanker nodded but he wasn't really paying attention. He wanted to ask her about Leather Jacket. He wanted to find out what was going on between them. He was afraid to ask in case his jealousy might beam through yet again in luminous green.

He sipped his coffee wondering how he might broach the subject when Lucy did it for him.

"I'm sorry about Denis."

"No, it's fine. I mean no sweat Lu. It's cool!"

"No, it's not. I should have told you. I saw you peeping out of the window. It wasn't fair. Anyway, I just went out with him as a friend. He asked me to a film and I went... But nothing happened. I mean we just talked. We had a long chat. He's a nice guy, Tanker. And he's not what you think he is."

Tanker said nothing. Ever since Yeoman had got into trouble over the drugs he was convinced that Denis Cummins had to have been involved. It all seemed to fit into place. Yeoman was friendly with this new rich kid. Yeoman kept it a secret from him. Yeoman got busted. Tanker didn't have to be Perry Mason to figure out the connection.

"Denis has nothing to do with drugs, Tanker."

Tanker gulped his coffee. How did Lucy know what he was thinking?

"He came to St Peter's not because he got thrown out of his last school but because his father refused to pay out the fees for his private school. Denis flunked the Junior Cert. One B, two Ds, three Es and... you'll like this one... an F in maths."

Tanker nodded his approval. An F in maths elevated Denis in his estimation. Lucy continued.

"His old fellow was as mad as hell. Told him there was no way he was going to fork out three grand a year for results like that. His father is originally from the northside and went to Peter's himself. He's one of these self-made men and he's always going on about how tough it was for him growing up. So Denis said he was sick of hearing about it and enrolled in Peter's himself."

"Wow! You mean he chose to go to Peter's. He must be thick! No wonder he flunked the Junior!"

"Anyway, Tanker, I can assure you that whatever else you think of Denis don't think of him as some kind of junkie or pusher. He's clean. He smokes ciggies. That's his only vice!"

"But I thought it was his fault that Yeoman got mixed up in the drugs. I thought he was a pusher too."

"Wrong again. Yeoman tried to sell Denis dope. He thought that because Denis was well-off he might be a good customer. Denis tried to put him straight. Kept telling him how dangerous it all was!"

Tanker felt stupid. Wrong again. How come he could never grasp things instead of grabbing the tail end all the time? At least tonight he had spent some time with Lucy. He wasn't feeling bitter any more. That was something. He finished his coffee and said goodnight. Lucy kissed him sisterly on the cheek. Tanker wanted to hold her and kiss her back in a non-brotherly way. But he resisted. It wasn't the right time.

"Don't worry, Tom. There's nothing happening between Denis and me. As they say in the movies, we're just good friends."

Tanker smiled. That was something too. Things were looking up.

He fell asleep listening to REM again. This time it was a tape he had made of end to end *Shiny Happy People*. Nothing else. Just the one track of over and over again for ninety minutes. It was colourful, cheerful, upbeat and strong. It made him feel as if nothing really mattered. Just for tonight nothing did.

Chapter 18

The Biker Strikes Again

It was Friday morning and Tanker was up early. It was mid-term the following week so he was enjoying that last day before the break feeling.

He was facing an English test later that morning and he wanted to read a short story before breakfast. He liked to read in the morning. It was always the best time to soak things in. He loved to lie there listening to the sounds outside. Footsteps on the courtyard, people saying their good-byes, milk bottles rattling to attention on doorsteps, cars pulling up or pulling away and whistling. So many people whistle in the morning. It made him feel snug.

He liked the idea in Junior Cert English that he was able to pick his own stories. Miss Lehane gave him a list of stories and he read the ones that he liked. The ones he hated he could skip. That made sense to Tanker. It was a pity the same rule didn't apply to maths. He would be quite happy doing long multiplication and forgetting all about algebra and simultaneous equations. He opened his book and began to read. As he did he heard his father's voice calling him.

"Are you up, Tank?"

"I'm reading. What are you doing up so early? It's only half past six?"

"Come on up and have a cup of tea with me. I'll tell you then."

Tanker threw on his jeans and sweatshirt and brought his book with him to the kitchen. Tom Kelly Senior stood with the teapot ready to pour. He was dressed in a shirt and tie in which Tanker reckoned he must have been married. He looked like an old shabby photograph brought to life.

"How do I look? Smart, eh?"

"Er... " Tanker didn't want to hurt his feelings. "You

look different that's for sure. But why the shirt and tie?"

"A job!" His father's face beamed with excitement.

"Ah no, Dad! You said you were going to go straight this time. You promised. Mam will go ape! She won't forgive you again!"

"No, Tank! It's straight up. That guard who called. Sergeant Donnelly. The guy you saved. He got me fixed up. He's got this contact who fixes up ex-pris... "

He stopped short of saying the word.

" ...people like myself. I must go down and see the gaffer this morning."

"A real job?"

"Yeah, great isn't it?"

"What as?"

"Security guard."

"A security guard! You! Come off it, Dad!"

Tanker wanted to laugh but he resisted the temptation. "Why not? I've been sort of doing it for years... only the other way round! It'll be five nights on, five nights off. The money sounds good. He wants to see me this morning to show me around in daylight."

"Nightwork? Real nightwork?"

"Don't be smart! I told you both I was going straight and this is it! So what do you think?"

"I think if you show up looking like that you'll give them all a good laugh!" Ann Kelly had just come into the kitchen. She stared at her husband in disbelief. "Go on into the bedroom and put on your jeans and sweater. It's a watchman's job you've got, not a part as an extra in the re-make of *Gone With The Wind*."

"You don't like it?"

"I loved it twenty years ago. Now go off and change!"

Her voice was not angry. Tanker was pleased with how they seemed to be getting along. As Tom Kelly went to carry out his wife's instructions Tanker smiled at his mother.

"Great, isn't it, Mam?"

"Yeah. Let's hope he can keep it up."

After school that day Tanker was feeling upbeat. The mid-term break always began with a half-day. He asked Yeoman to go for a game of snooker. Lucy said she'd come down later and play the winner. The two lads grinned. She always said that but she never showed up.

Tanker broke and potted a red with the black hanging over the bottom right. He loved when that happened. As he lined up to take his pot Lucy came running in. She was upset about something.

"What is it, Lucy?" he put down his cue and put his hands on to her shoulders.

"This guy on a motorbike just grabbed me in Jones' Lane. He must have been following us from school. A big huge ape of a man in leather jacket and a crash helmet. I think he might have been the guy who attacked you, Tanker!"

Tanker nodded, hoping that there weren't two similar apes on motorbikes.

"He asked me if I was friend of yours, Yeoman. He told me to give you a message. The Queen wants her cash. The guy'll collect it himself tomorrow morning at eight sharp. Leave it in a coke can on the first bin outside the shed-house at exactly one minute to eight. If he isn't there by five-past pick it up and try again at exactly one minute to nine."

"Damn! I don't have it! I don't have the bloody two hundred quid! What am I going to do?"

"He said that if you screw up he'll come and get you, Yeoman! He's a scary guy!"

"What am I going to do, Tank?"

Tanker didn't know what to say. His immediate reaction was to go to the guards with Yeoman and let them know what was happening but he was afraid that this might only make things worse. This Biker guy was only the messenger boy for the Queen. If he was caught she would simply send another. There was no easy escape route for his friend. There was no easy answer. Maybe if he could try and explain what had happened at school. Maybe if the Queen would agree to take what Yeoman owed her in instalments.

"You can have the money we make at Sean Bradys. Surely Celia will help you out too."

"Celia's only on a trainee nurse's wage. She gives most of that up at home. The rest goes on keeping that crock of a car going."

"Don't panic, Yeoman. I'll go with you in the morning. We'll think of something." Tanker tried to reassure him.

"I'll be there too. Maybe a bit of feminine charm might help." Lucy was lending her support.

"Dealing with the Queen doesn't involve feminine charm Lucy," Yeoman told her as he abandoned his game of snooker and placed his cue on the table.

They met at seven-thirty the following morning. Yeoman pushed the note they had composed the night before into the empty coke can. The message on it was simple.

> *Tell Q I will pay her back over the next ten weeks. Please meet me in the shed-house now where I will tell you how and we can make arrangements."*

It was more of a begging letter than a note but they each felt that it sounded genuine. It read as if here was a guy who had screwed up and was prepared to put things right. Here was someone who wasn't going to run away and hide. They hoped that the Queen would read it this way too.

Tanker and Lucy watched from behind a pillar on the first floor balcony. At exactly one minute to eight Yeoman placed the can on the edge of the bin as requested and made his way to the shed-house. The Biker was bang on time. He looked every bit as mean as the night he hammered Tanker.

"Christ, he's big !" whispered Tanker.

"A gorilla in a previous existence." Lucy wasn't trying to be funny.

The Biker picked up the can in his huge leather gloved hand. From a flat behind him Tanker heard the pips from a radio signalling that it was eight o'clock and time for the news. The Biker shook the can and grimaced. Without removing his glove, he fished out the note. Neither Tanker nor Lucy had to be able to lip-read to guage his reaction. Stifling an angry growl he drop-kicked the can into the air. It clattered to a halt in the middle of the car-park disturbing only a flock of gulls which had landed for some sparse dawn-time pickings.

Sighing deeply, the Biker looked around to see if anybody had noticed him before leaving his bike and hurrying to the shed-house.

"Let's go, Lu! I think there might be trouble!"

"That's a bit of an under-statement, Tank."

"We can pretend that we're going in. It might distract the Biker from killing Yeoman!"

They were just in time to hear Yeoman's pleas.

"Listen, mister, I'm serious. I gave out the gear in school but they didn't pay up! The guards are on to me. They want names. I can't do any more deals!"

"You knew the rules! No cash no hash!"

"Yeah but..."

Yeoman's attempt at a plea was interrupted by the outbreak of a scuffle. Tanker gritted his teeth hard. Suddenly there was a loud whacking sound followed by a reflex-like groan.

"Ugh!"

Tanker suspected the "ugh" was a result of the Biker's knee connecting with Yeoman's groin. He winced in imagined pain as terror now ran through him. He knew he couldn't stand back and let his friend take this beating but at the same time he had already suffered at the hands, feet and head of the Biker. Did he really want to go through all that again? He found himself in that awful fight-or-flight position. The friend in him wanted to jump in and do battle. The coward in him wanted to run for miles. Luckily he didn't have to make the choice.

As Tanker and Lucy hid nervously behind the pillar at the entrance to the shed-house, the Biker came out holding the back of his neck with both hands. He seemed to be in great pain but continued to shout threateningly.

"This isn't over yet, mate! I'll get you! And your friends! The fat poxfaced excuse for a human being and the girl with the dartboard face. They're in it with you, Dunne! I saw them spying from the balcony. I'll get them too. Just you wait, Dunne! Just you wait!"

Tanker couldn't believe it. He knew Yeoman was tough but there was no way he expected him to double up the Biker. As the Biker revved up to make a hasty exit Yeoman came out calling after him.

"I was the one that wanted to be reasonable!" he roared hoping to be heard over the bike's engine. "You were the one who wanted the aggro, not me!"

Behind Yeoman there came a series of smoke rings.

"Christ, Denis! How did you get here?" Tanker was stunned.

"Lucy phoned me and told me about your plans last night. I figured you might need a little help."

Yeoman slapped him on the shoulder.

"You were sensational, man! Out of sight! One thump to the back of the head and splat!"

"The Tae Kwon Do lessons come in handy every now and then!"

Tanker stared at Denis in disbelief. Immediately the contempt he had felt for him up until now evaporated into sheer admiration. This guy had guts.

"Come on up to my flat, we can have some breakfast and talk about what we'll do next. You can come too, Denis."

"Thanks, but are you sure your folks won't mind?"

"They're both at work."

Lucy and Yeoman stared at Tanker in oh-no-not-again fashion.

"It's okay. My old fellow has a real job now. Security guard at the industrial park!"

"Your old man working as a security guard! That's a bit of a joke isn't it!"

"Yeah, Yeoman! Like ha bloody ha! Come on. We've got to go and see about our own jobs at eleven."

Tanker made tea and toast as they sat in the kitchen wondering how soon the Queen would react to the Biker's news. Yeoman reckoned that she'd send him back with a whole gang the next time and sort them all out. Lucy thought the Queen might be a little more tactful.

"What good will getting us all done in do? She'll have to pay these guys to come around here. In the end it will cost her more than you owe her. I mean it's only two hundred quid. It's not that much really."

Yeoman stared at her wide-eyed.

"It might as well be two million when you haven't bloody well got it."

Denis lit a cigarette and blew some more rings before speaking. This used to drive Tanker crazy before. He remembered the first time he saw him in the disco and how he thought of him as being a big chief sending smoke signals. Now, however, he couldn't understand why he had made such a big deal about it all.

"What do you think, Denis?"

"I don't think this Biker will tell the Queen about the thump I gave him. I reckon he'll say that he gave you a fright and that you'll pay up the next time. I mean a big animal like him isn't going to admit to her that he got scared off by a slap, is he? I reckon you'll be safe enough for a week or so. He'll probably tell her that you want to pay in instalments. She might buy that. I mean she hasn't much choice."

Tanker thought this made a lot of sense. He wasn't forgetting, however, that Sean Brady had asked him about the Queen. If she had been involved in the burning down of Joe's Diner then there was no knowing what she might be capable of. The Queen was a dangerous customer. They couldn't presume that she would be in any way lenient to Yeoman or at this stage to any of them.

Chapter 19

Saturday in North Main Street

Working at Sean Brady's was a pure doddle. All they had to do was deliver some parcels, make tea, answer the phone, put photographs and negatives into envelopes and listen to the radio. Sean provided them with a mountain bike for the deliveries which were nearly all in or around the city centre. Most of the clients gave a tip on delivery. Some only gave twenty pence but most gave fifty or a pound.

The workshop was mind-blowing. On the walls Sean had the most amazing collection of framed photographs and posters. Both Tanker and Yeoman liked the look of the computer which did the poster typesetting. Sean did that work himself but he promised to show them both how it was done. He had a dark room too where all the prints were Róisín developed all the prints.

They finished at around three o'clock. They were delighted when Sean asked them to come back again on Monday, the first day of their mid-term break, to help with the backlog. In fact they were hoping that he would find more work for them for the rest of their week off.

Back out on the street it took some time for their eyes to readjust to the daylight. Tanker dug deep into his pockets and pulled out his money which he counted into Yeoman's hand.

"Ten, twenty, twenty one, twenty two, twenty three, hold it!"

He pulled some change from his back pocket, "And sixty pence! Twenty-three pounds sixty pence. That's sixteen quid for four hours at four quid an hour and seven-sixty tips. Not bad, eh?"

"I can't take all this, Tank!" Yeoman was grovelling again.

"Yes, you can."

"But you own at least half of it!"

"If it makes you feel better we can say you owe it to me. I'll keep an account. I'll even charge you interest."

"Interest!"

"Only joking, butt-head."

"Here! At least take a fiver."

"Okay, if it makes you feel better! Come on, let's go and meet Denis and Lucy."

They had arranged to meet in a pool hall off the North Main Street. Lucy was at the table when they came in. Denis stood leaning against the jukebox, holding his cue as Lucy potted the stripes one by one. Tanker was amazed.

"I didn't know you could play pool like that, Lucy!"

"I never knew myself until now!"

Lucy steadied herself up to pot the black and win the game. She lashed the cue ball off three cushions before it smashed against the black ball, rattling it into the top right pocket. She held the cue aloft with both hands.

"Yippee! Next challenger, please! Place your money and take your chance!"

"I'll take you on, Lucy!" said Yeoman confidently.

"Just be careful. I must have been a shark in a previous existence!"

"Not with those nose-rings, you weren't!"

Denis told Tanker he had some news for him. They went to the coffee dock to get cokes. They sat drinking from the ice cold cans as Lucy allowed Yeoman to break.

"Sorry about being a total prat, Denis. I had you all wrong." Tanker found the apology a lot easier than he had feared.

"You? A total prat? Never!"

"No, it's just we got off to a bad start. The night at the disco when you came over to ask for a light and then later in Joe's when you came in to get chips. I thought you were a bit of a know-all."

"Yeah?"

"Well, sort of! I mean to say, you had a taxi waiting outside! Come on now, a taxi! None of the friends I hang around with travel in taxis."

"Yeah, well none of your friends have fathers who own Cork Mini-Cabs. When I don't have the bike with me I phone home. It's a lot easier for one of the drivers to pick me up than to walk three miles up to Cnoc Barra."

"Your father owns Cork Mini-Cabs! Wow!"

"Your father has been in the nick! Wow!"

Denis was teasing but Tanker got the message.

"Get a grip, Tanker. I can't help it if my father's rich any more than you can help the fact that your father isn't. It doesn't matter. Anyway I didn't want to talk to you about our old fellas. I thought you might be interested in knowing something about a neighbour of mine."

"A neighbour of yours! How would I know anything about anybody living in Cnoc... " Tanker's voice trailed off as the thought struck him, "The Queen?"

"Spot on! Ms Mary Glynn. She bought a house up by us last year. The locals are going mad about it. Having a drug baron as a neighbour isn't going to put the value of your house up. Anyway I don't know a lot about her except for what she looks like. She keeps to herself. If you and Yeoman want to come to my place tomorrow I'll show you her house."

"Actually we're playing Mayfield tomorrow at twelve. The pitch isn't too far from Cnoc Barra. We can call over to your place after."

"I'll go to the match myself and see you afterwards."

Tanker was amazed at how wrong he had been about Denis. He felt so foolish now when he thought about all the stupid names he had called him in the past. He was just about to apologise again when he stopped himself. Once was enough. There was no point in grovelling.

Lucy came over and asked for another challenger. Yeoman

stood with his head bowed.

"I didn't get to pot a ball!" he moaned. "You've been taking lessons!"

"Yeah right, Yeoman! Like you lose a game of pool and all of a sudden there's a special school just to teach girls how to beat you!"

Tanker laughed. He wasn't letting Yeoman get away with this one. Losing to Lucy Higgins at pool was going to be a tough one to live down for someone who commanded respect in the Blackpool Snooker Club.

"Yeah well, I don't know how she learned so fast!" Yeoman was a sore loser.

"It's called natural ability!"

"It's called beginner's luck!" Tanker told her as he took the cue from Yeoman's hand. "Come on Lucy I'll beat you and you can break!"

Tanker headed down to the pool table leaving Denis to tell Yeoman of their plans for the morning.

Chapter 20

Frustration

Tanker hadn't played soccer since the day after his father was released from prison when they beat Denis's team St Bonaventure's four-nil. It was great to get back on to the pitch again. After all the hassle of the past three weeks it was great to put on his goalkeeping gear and get out there diving around in the mud. On the line he could hear his mother and father cheering his every save. Lucy was screeching his name all the time even when the play was up the other end of the pitch.

"Come on, Tanker! Great stuff, Tank!"

In the past this used to embarrass him no end. This morning however he didn't mind at all. Winning one-nil also made him feel good.

After the match Yeoman, Lucy and Denis were waiting for him.

"Come on, Tanker, I'm dying to see this place!" Yeoman was raring to go.

Yeoman had decided he was going to get to the Queen before she got to him. He had told Tanker that he wasn't going to wait until he was paid another visit by the Biker. The next time Denis mightn't be around to exhibit his black-belt skills. He knew it would be risky calling up to see her directly but he felt that if he could just tell her to her face that he would be willing to pay her she might leave him alone.

"There it is, boys!" announced Denis. "The Palace of the Queen. Otherwise known as Mary Glynn's Gaff. Don't stare, Yeoman. Those walls have ears and eyes!"

If it wasn't a palace it certainly was a mansion. It was huge. It reminded Tanker of one of those stately homes full of black and white-clad servants and an officious-looking butler. Yeoman just stood and stared in amazement, muttering a long version of wow. Denis didn't want them either hanging around the place or staring in. The house was surrounded by a huge perimeter wall with surveillance cameras positioned to monitor any loiterers.

"Just pretend we're walking past, lads. She'll pick up anybody behaving suspiciously from those cameras." Denis was being careful not to get into any unnecessary trouble with his new neighbour Ms Glynn.

Yeoman was deflated. He had told Tanker of his plan just to walk right on up to the front door and ring the bell. Tanker could spot his friend's disappointment instantly.

"There's no way she'd allow you through the gates of that place, Yeoman. You'll have to wait until she contacts you. Don't worry. We won't leave you on your own."

"You weren't seriously thinking of going in there were you Yeoman?" Lucy asked him as they made the long trek back to the Mansions.

"Nah. Not really!" Tanker said nothing. Part of him knew that Yeoman hadn't given up on the idea completely. Lucy shook her head as she pondered what might have happened.

"Jesus! That would have been wild. You'd have been eaten alive. You'd have come back as a pound of sausage-meat in your next existence!"

"Lucy, stop going on about my next existence! I'm doing my best to hold on to my present one!"

As Lucy went into her flat Yeoman called Tanker.

"Thanks for staying quiet. I would have felt stupid if Denis and Lucy had known that I wanted to go and see the Queen in person!"

"No sweat, Yeoman. See you later. Don't go out of the flats without me."

"Sure. Thanks."

When he got home his mother was serving up chicken with roast spuds and gravy.

"That smells great, Mam! Good match, wasn't it?"

"Yes, son, you played well."

"Thanks. What did you think, Dad?"

There was no answer. From underneath the pages of his *Sunday World* Tom Kelly let out a gentle snore.

"He's worn out from that new job of his!" his mother explained. "He should have gone to bed when he came back this morning but he had a quick snooze and headed off to see the match. I suppose he's trying to make up for lost time."

Ann Kelly served three dinners and put one in the oven covering it with the lid of a saucepan. She sat with her son in the kitchen as her husband slept on. It was a long time since Tanker had seen her as happy and relaxed. It made him feel good.

"Dad's been really good this time, hasn't he, Mam?" Tanker was anxious to find out how she felt. It wasn't often he got a chance to talk to her on his own. In fact ever since the row he hadn't really spoken much to her at all.

"He's doing better than I thought he would, son."

"He likes the job, doesn't he?"

"He loves it. You'd swear he was in charge of security at Fort Knox!"

"With him working you might be able to give up your cleaning job in the bank!"

"You must be mad, Tom! I don't trust him that much. This time next week he might be back inside again!"

"You don't believe that, Mam, do you?"

Ann Kelly looked at her son. She didn't want to say any more. So far so good was her attitude to her husband's behaviour since his release but she was going to take things slowly. She wasn't going to tempt fate. It was time to change the subject.

"I wrote to the corporation about those bloody stairs by the way. I told them that you were nearly killed and that I was very seriously considering taking legal action against them!"

"Ah, Mam! There was no need to say that!"

"Why not? It's true isn't it?"

Tanker filled his mouth with hot potato. It made it easier to nod a lie.

"I didn't say anything about that drunken sod, Benny. I know he does nothing but I don't want to lose him his job."

"Oh right, Mam, yeah. That would be going a bit to far. Poor old Benny is harmless."

Tanker sighed as he felt that was the end of the affair. She had written her letter and that was that. Now please change the subject!

"Your dad and I are taking the train to Mallow tomorrow. We're staying over. We want you to come. It's been ages since you've seen Aunt Sheila."

Aunt Sheila! Red Alert! The aunt from hell! He had to think fast.

"Ah, Mam! Sean Brady wants me to work. It's a great job and I don't want to lose it!"

"Nonsense. You can ring and explain. With us both working now there's no need for you to think you should have to earn anything!"

"But I love this work, Mam. In fact I think I'd like to get into photography when I leave school."

"Hmm, I don't know."

"Besides, I don't want to let Sean down. He wants both Yeoman and myself to go in but there will only be one job there at the end of the day. I don't want him to think that Yeoman is more reliable than me!"

"Him! More reliable than you! Eamon Dunne more reliable than my son!" she shrieked, causing her husband to suddenly snore louder. She lowered her voice. "That fellow couldn't live in your shadow!"

Tanker grinned. He felt guilty using Yeoman to get out of

the visit to Mallow but there was no way he was going to suffer an overnight stay with Aunt Sheila. She never stopped talking. Her house reeked of cabbage and there were cats crawling all over the place. Five minutes with Aunt Sheila was serious headache country.

"How's Yeoman getting on with the guards?" Ann Kelly asked as she planted another slice of chicken breast on his plate.

God, from one sticky situation to another! This was turning into a gruelling lunch.

"Mmm... they've let him off with a warning. They told him that if he's ever asked to sell dope again he must go straight to them with names."

"Yeah, I was talking to his father after mass. He said the same thing. He's been a very lucky lad, hasn't he?"

"How do you mean?"

"To get away with it. I mean to say other lads who get involved in drugs have been shot or beaten to death with baseball bats. It was a good lesson for him. At least he got out before it all got out of hand. He got away with a warning. He could have been killed."

Even though the chicken was delicious it began to stick in Tanker's throat. If only things were as simple as his mother thought. If only...

Chapter 21

Bingo!

Monday morning in the studio was hectic.

"Yeoman, if you take the bike there's a delivery of posters for Murphy's Brewery. Just hand them to the guy at the gate and wait for him to get the invoice signed. While he's doing that, Tom, will you sort those photos? They've been there since the week of the funeral. Róisín does all the developing for me when I'm away but I'd forgotten all about them until now. There's a list of customers here. Ring them up and tell them their stuff is ready. If you finish up before I get back don't forget to turn on the alarm and throw the keys back in through the letterbox."

Sean Brady was busy packing a portfolio case. He was going off for the afternoon to meet a client and was giving his instructions before he left. It was only the second day the lads were working for him but he was pleased at how easily they seemed to be picking things up.

"Oh, by the way. This guy Duffy was on to me. Apparently he left in some snaps while I was away. He sounded pretty mad that we were locked up when he came to collect them. Anyway try and find his first and give him a bell. I'm sure they're among that lot somewhere. Oh, and don't forget to do the post before five. See you!"

Sean headed out the door dragging his case. Yeoman took the bike out of the store and hopped on. He perched a huge parcel on the basket in front of the handlebars and wobbled his way out onto the street, leaving Tanker all alone in the workshop.

Tanker decided to start with the photograph packaging. He loved looking at other people's photographs. They were all so similar. Loads of them had children doing typical children-in-photograph things: sitting at birthday parties, blowing out candles, standing in front of Christmas trees or simply grinning, widely mouthing the word "cheese". Other collections were of wedding parties with brides and grooms holding hands, wedding guests standing stiffly wearing floppy hats or elderly men wearing tight-fitting suits trying to hold back their beer bellies. More packets were of people standing in front of houses and cars, or very often simply pictures of houses and cars.

He had just packaged yet another bunch of happy wedding snaps and negatives when he reached for the next pile. It was a people and houses pile. However, when he looked again at the first snap he froze. It was as if the world had suddenly ground to a halt. The first snap in this bunch was of Joe. He was crossing the street to the Diner and seemed unaware that he was being photographed. The next three shots were of the Diner, one from the front, another from the rear and the third from the laneway to the side of the building. The rest of the photographs didn't mean much to Tanker. They were of people he didn't recognise. However, there were some of a pub he knew. Maybe this pub was next in line for an attack.

As he was trying to consider his next move, Yeoman came back from the Brewery.

"Great bike that! I was there and back in ten minutes! What's up with you?"

Tanker handed him the snaps. Yeoman shook his head.

"How did they get here? Who handed them in?"

"There's a name on the envelope. I think it says Paul Duffy. There's a mobile phone number too. I think I'll dial it and ask for him. I'll tell him his snaps are ready. Hopefully he'll call in today."

"Aren't you going to tell Sean first?"

"He won't be back until about five."

Yeoman picked up the receiver and handed it to Tanker.

"Go on! Dial it!"

Tanker tapped his finger nervously on the counter as the phone rang shrilly on the other side.

"Hello. Duffy." The voice was sharp but instantly recognisable. Tanker had to keep calm. He had to sound as if he was dealing with just another customer on the list.

"Mr Duffy, this is Tom from Sean Brady's Photography and Printers. Sorry about the delay in processing your photos but we were closed for a few days last week and some films were mislaid. We have your prints ready now though if you'd like to call and collect them."

"Right. I'll be there at around four o'clock."

"Thank you, Mr Duffy"

Tanker's worst suspicions were confirmed. The voice at the other end of the telephone belonged to the Biker. He would have recognised that growl anywhere.

"The Biker! He'll eat me without salt. I better stay out of sight when he calls." Yeoman was going to make himself scarce. "But he'll probably recognise you too. What are you going to do?"

"I don't know. I don't think he saw much of me the night he beat me up. It was very dark and I was all wrapped up!"

"But what if he's been watching us? He might have seen you the day he followed Lucy." Yeoman was getting paranoid.

"Just stay cool, Yeoman. He won't expect to see me here. He'll be too interested in seeing his snaps to notice me. Besides, I won't exactly look him in the eye."

Tanker had the packet of photographs ready for the Biker. He had removed the four pictures and negatives of Joe and the Diner and placed them in an envelope. Then he sorted through some old negatives which he found in a bin in the corner of the workshop. He looked through them until he settled on four blanks. He put these in with the other negatives. On the envelope jacket he wrote "Twenty/Twenty

Four". On the back of the envelope was a list of possible reasons for sub-standard prints. Tanker read through them and ticked "Poor Light" as the reason for the first four photographs being absent from the packet.

"Will he fall for that?" Yeoman was still going through paranoia.

"I won't ask any questions. I'll just hand him the packet and ask for the money."

At exactly four o'clock the Biker strode up to the counter. He had ignored the request on the door for motorcyclists to remove helmets before entry but Tanker didn't feel like pointing out the house rules to him.

"Photographs for Duffy!" His bark was muffled by the scarf he wore around his mouth.

Tanker was pretending to clean out a cupboard under the counter. He got up and went into the darkroom where Yeoman was hiding and returned with the envelope which he handed to the Biker. He was careful to keep his face down and had donned a baseball cap which he thought made him look completely different.

"Four pounds please," he said in what he hoped was an English accent.

The Biker slammed four pound coins on the counter and left. Tanker watched him through the glass panel of the door. He didn't look at the photographs. He simply shoved them inside his jacket and hopped on to his bike. In seconds he was out of sight with the roar of his five hundred cc engine still buzzing in the busy Monday mid-afternoon air.

Tanker was confused as to why the Biker would want these pictures. Obviously the shots would have been used in planning the fire, but why take such risks? Surely this was dangerous evidence to leave lying around.

"Not really, Tank." Yeoman was doing his Sherlock Holmes bit. "I mean, do you really look at the photos when you're packing them?"

"I do, actually."

"Yeah, well that's because we've just started this job. I'm sure Róisín just glances at the prints. After a while they all begin to look the same."

Tanker nodded. It was true. Even after the first few packages he had made up, it had struck him how similar everybody's snaps were. For any one developing these prints for years there would have been nothing unusual or sinister in Duffy's collection.

"I suppose you're right. He mightn't have known that the shots of Joe were even on that roll. I mean most of them were of that pub. Anyway, look, it's getting late. I'd better get the post done. You stay here and hold the fort."

"But what if the Biker comes back?"

"Chill out, Yeoman. I'll only be five minutes! Lock the door if it makes you feel better. I'll knock the first three bars of *Brick in the Wall* when I come back!"

"No way, Tanker! I'm not staying here on my own. We'll lock up here and do the post together. Then we can head straight to Pizza Place."

Tanker nodded in agreement and set about locking up. He sensed that his friend was terrified that the Biker would return. Maybe it was a good idea for them both to go and not risk that happening. Besides, if Duffy was to come back there was a greater chance that he would recognise him this time.

He dialled in the alarm code, 12 06 88, which Sean had told him had been one of the most famous dates in Irish sporting history. Ireland 1 England 0 in the European Championships in Germany. Tanker was too young to remember the game but he had seen the goal on telly several times and as he clicked in the numbers he replayed it in his mind.

The alarmed emitted its whining buzz.

"Let's go, Yeoman! Thirty seconds to lock up!"

For a Monday afternoon there was a larger than usual crowd in the city. As most schools were closed for the week, hordes of young people were wandering in and out of the shops or gathering in the seating areas of the pedestrianised streets. As they walked towards the General Post Office at the end of Oliver Plunkett Street, Yeoman was continuously looking over his shoulder.

"Relax, Yeoman! You're making me nervous!"

"Sorry, Tank! I just have this feeling that we're being followed."

"Yeah, Yeoman! Look behind you. There are at least two hundred people."

"You know what I mean! Every time I hear a bike engine I think it's him."

"Look, I'll nip over to get rid of this lot and you head on to Pizza Place. Lucy is probably already there picking the ham off the pizzas. Tell her I'll join you in about ten minutes. That is if you're not too scared to walk up Shandon Street on your own?"

"Don't be daft!"

"Are you sure you don't want me to hold your hand?"

"Get lost, Tank! See you later."

Yeoman jogged down a side-street as Tanker crossed the street to post his bundle of letters. Outside the Post Office he saw a tall garda standing on duty. Tanker sorted through his bundle and posted all but one.

"Excuse me, Garda!"

The garda eyed him suspiciously.

"Do you know Sergeant Ted Donnelly?"

"I do. He's my boss." The look was still suspicious. "Why do you ask?"

"Well, I have this letter for him. I deliver stuff for a photographer and I noticed his name on the envelope. If you handed it to him he might have it sooner."

Tanker handed him the envelope. As he read the address Tanker could see that his initial suspicion had yielded to a smile.

"That's very thoughtful of you, son! I'll leave it in his mail tray when I get off duty in an hour. Who shall I say it's from... ?"

"Brady's Photography and Printers."

Tanker didn't stay around to explain any further. He thanked the garda who put the envelope inside his jacket.

He quickened his pace. He was late. He had arranged to meet Lucy at five in Pizza Place. He was already five minutes behind and it would take him at least another fifteen to walk there. He crossed the road and began to run down a narrow laneway. Unlike the busy street he had just left the laneway was deserted. Suddenly he heard the roar of a motorbike behind him.

He looked back only to see the Biker braking hard as he pushed his front wheel across his path.

"So!" he growled. "You thought you could fool me, did you, Thomas Kelly! Putting on that stupid accent! Do you take me for an idiot?

"No sir... "

Tanker stared in disbelief as the Biker got off his bike and pushed him up against a wall.

"I wasn't trying to fool you... "

"Where are those snaps?"

"Snaps?"

"The ones you left out of the packet!"

"Oh those! They're probably in the studio! They didn't come out very well! Poor light I think! Sean doesn't allow us to give out sub-standard... "

"What did you say to that cop?"

Tanker froze. Duffy had seen him talking to the garda outside the post office. What if he saw him handing him that envelope?

"What cop?"

"Don't mess me around! I saw you talking to a cop outside... "

"Oh him! That cop... I asked him the time of the next collection... That's all... He started asking me what I was doing with all those letters and I told him I was working... He started giving me grief... about being too young to work... and that I should be in school... and I told him I was on mid-term... and that I was only helping my uncle... "

"I hope that was all you said!"

"It was, Mr Duffy! Honest! Please let me go! You're hurting me!"

Tanker's plea was cut short as the Biker slapped him across the mouth with his leather-clad fist. Tanker tasted blood. His tongue was cut and he could feel the jagged edge of a chipped back tooth. He winced in pain as the Biker let him flop to the ground.

"Now, Thomas! No more games. You and I are going back to your little shop and you are going to give me those photos!"

"Okay! I'll get them for you! I know where they are!"

The Biker handed Tanker a helmet which he had taken from a plastic container on the back of his bike.

"Hop on! And stay on!" he barked. "Don't try anything funny or I'll get you! And I'll get that poxy friend of yours and your little baldy girlfriend."

Tanker sat onto the back of the bike. As they sped down the laneway he was overcome with terror. The photographs were not back in the studio but Duffy must have thought that they were. Obviously he hadn't seen him handing over the envelope to the garda. That was a relief. But for how long could he keep this up? Once they would get back to the studio there was no way that he was going to be able to continue this game of bluff with Duffy. He would have to try to make a run for it.

Duffy stopped the bike at the traffic lights at an intersection. He was waiting in the inside lane to turn left into Patrick Street from Merchants Quay. Tanker waited for more cars to pull up alongside them in the other three lanes.

As the lights changed from red to green Duffy revved the bike, shoved the throttle into gear and began to make his left turn. As they moved forward, Tanker jumped off, kicking the bike in the process and sending Duffy sprawling headfirst onto the sidewalk and into the path of a bewildered group of American tourists. Tanker leap-frogged over the bonnets of several cars as he made his getaway, to the tune of blaring car-horns, in the direction of Shandon Street.

Chapter 22

No Pizza

Tanker didn't even try to explain. He saw Yeoman sitting on his own in Pizza Place.

"Out!" he roared.

Yeoman instantly knew what was happening.

"Where's Lucy?"

"I don't know. The waitress said she was here but she got tired of waiting. Is it Duffy?"

"Yeah! Come on, let's go!"

"Leg it to Horgan's! Hurry – he won't be far behind!"

The two ran out of the restaurant, the waitress screaming after them.

"You haven't paid!"

"We haven't eaten!" Tanker told her breathlessly as he pushed Yeoman out the door ahead of him.

They sprinted past the Cathedral and down into Blackpool. As they neared Horgan's Yard, Tanker was sure he could hear the roar of Duffy's bike behind him. Horgan's was a closed-down scrapyard where Tanker and Yeoman used to hang out when they were younger, making their own cars from the discarded parts and wheels. Today, however, they were certainly not calling in to play engines and drivers.

They scrambled over the high wall and hid behind the shell of an old tractor.

When he had got his breath back Tanker told Yeoman what had happened. He left out the bit about giving the snaps to the garda. He wasn't sure how Yeoman would react to that. The gardaí weren't high up on Yeoman's list of favourite authority figures. He would tell him later when things were calmer.

Neither of them was sure as to what to do next. They spoke in whispers, each fearing that the Biker was closing in on them all the time.

"Let's give it an hour. Then we'll head to the Garda Station in Blackpool," Tanker suggested.

"No, not the cops!" snapped Yeoman. "Leave them out of it! No, we'll go back to the studio and get the snaps! Right, Tanker?"

Tanker gulped.

"Er... I reckon it might be a bit dodgy going back there. Anyway it's locked up and the alarm is on. I threw the keys in through the letterbox."

"Damn!"

"Maybe we should head back to your flat, Yeoman. We might be safer there. Your mam and dad are expecting me to stay over tonight anyway."

"I don't know about that. Duffy is probably watching the flats... "

"Denis!" Tanker said brightly. "We can give him a ring! He'll put us up for the night. His folks are away until tomorrow so himself and his sister are on their own!"

"Great! We'll hang on here for another while and then we can ring him from the payphone across the road!"

Tanker was relieved. They would have time to think in Denis's house. Maybe Denis would be able to convince Yeoman that going to the guards would be the best way out.

After an hour of lying behind the tractor Tanker reluctantly decided to brave it outside. He looked up and down the road. All seemed quiet. He crossed the road and entered the phone kiosk. He flicked through the pages of the directory and nervously fingered his way through the list of Cummins. At last he hit on the right one. Cummins, Cnoc Barra. Anxiously, he dialled the number. He heard the phone ringing on the other side. "Come on, Denis!" he whispered nervously to himself. "Pick the bloody thing up!"

His heart was pounding as the intermittent burr-burr filled his ear. Click!

"Hello?" It was Denis. Yes! Tanker thought as relief washed through him. His hand shook as he fumbled with the coin. He dropped it into the slot. He was just about to speak when a gloved hand reached in and calmly took the receiver from him.

"Hello, is that the Imperial Hotel?"

Tanker could hear Denis's distant voice telling the Biker that he had a wrong number.

The Biker replaced the receiver and grinned at Tanker.

"Silly boy, Thomas!" he hissed from behind his helmet. "I said no more games!"

He grabbed Tanker by his hair and bundled him into the back of a Hiace van. He climbed in himself and slammed the doors shut.

"Now, Thomas, it's time to pick up your friend! I believe he's hiding behind a Massey Ferguson!" Tanker swallowed hard. The Biker must have been watching them all the time.

"Horgan's Scrapyard!" he bellowed to the driver.

"You didn't seriously believe that you could get away from me, Thomas, did you?" He grinned at Tanker who was lying at his feet on the floor of the van. Tanker groaned as the Biker failed to resist the temptation to kick him in the ribs.

"That's for knocking me off me bike!"

At Horgan's the driver and another man got out. Seconds later the back doors were opened again and Yeoman was thrown in alongside Tanker.

"Heh!" The shout came from across the road. Tanker recognised it immediately. It was Lucy. Please, Lucy, thought Tanker, run away, get out of here, don't say another word, just run for God's sake, run! He should have known better.

"What are you doing? Leave him alone, you big bully!" she screamed.

The Biker ran across the road and grabbed her. Tanker

could hear her struggling but her screams were becoming more and more muffled. She was thrown, into the van and made to lie down next to Tanker.

"You saved me the trouble of looking for you later, sweetie!" the Biker sneered.

"Don't you sweetie me, you big asshole!"

"Now, *sweetie!*" Duffy growled. "One more sound out of you and I'll do some body-piercings of my own on you!" From a holder inside his jacket he pulled out a long-bladed knife. He ran the blade around the contours of her cheeks and under her chin, prodding the skin teasingly.

Lucy brought her finger to her lips in a not-another-word fashion.

"Good girl!" He pulled the knife slowly away and slid it back into its holder.

"Move!" Duffy roared as the driver shoved the van into gear and sped off.

"Stay down!" This time the roar was for them as he indicated that they should remain on the floor of the van.

"Are you okay?" Tanker whispered to Lucy.

"Quiet!" Another roar. Tanker felt another kick.

Lucy muttered a barely audible "yeah" as the van thundered noisily on its way.

When the van screeched to a halt, each of the three were grabbed and blindfolded. Their hands were bound tightly behind their backs and they were led across a gravelled surface into a building. Tanker shivered as he heard the aggressive barking of a dog. They were brought down what felt like stone steps, pushed into a room and made sit on the floor.

Tanker braced himself. His mind went back to that time when he accidentally kicked that wrong can and found himself the recipient of a pounding from the Biker. His tongue was still throbbing since the thump he had been given in the laneway earlier. Here we go again, he thought. He was surprised however when he felt the blindfold being yanked off his face and his hands released from the tight bandages with which they had been bound.

They were in a cellar. It was dark. The pungent smell of dampness hung heavily in the air. The Biker stood before them clutching one leather-clad hand in the other as if he was preparing to make a speech. Two other members of his gang stood beside him. One was holding a rottweiler on a long chain. The dog hissed angrily in the direction of the three, each hiss rewarded with a "good boy" from its handler.

"Now, Eamon and friends!" He stared coldly at each of them in turn. "You have been very naughty. You have made me very cross. And I know that one of you has something which belongs to me."

Tanker put his head down. The Biker strode towards him and put his finger to Tanker's chin, tilting his face so it met his own angry stare.

"I am going to leave you here until eight o'clock tomorrow morning. At that time I will return and you will get those pictures and negatives for me. My superior is not too pleased with you at all. In fact she is very disappointed. She wants to see her pictures tomorrow. Do I make myself clear?"

Tanker nodded. The dog started barking wildly. He was struggling to break free from the lead. Tanker could see saliva dripping from its raw red mouth as its teeth gleamed in the dim light of the room. This was not the time to argue.

"No problem, sir!" Yeoman was grovelling. "We'll find them for you! They're in the studio."

"Shut up, you little worm!"

He continued to stare at Tanker.

"You may have thought you were very clever, boy! But the day you think you've outsmarted me... " he paused as he spat out each word deliberately, "will... be... your... last! Comprendez?"

The dog was in a frenzy as if he agreed with every word

from the Biker. His handler moved closer to Tanker, holding him within inches of his face. Tanker could smell the beast's meaty breath as it panted at him. The Biker grabbed him once more.

"Understand?"

Tanker looked him straight in the eye for a second before nodding again and turning his face away.

"Good."

The three men and the dog left the cellar, slamming the door closed behind them. Their three captives heard the metal clicking as a key was turned in the lock. Then the dim light from the low-watt bulb hanging from the ceiling went out. They were alone in total darkness. For a few moments they were afraid to talk. Lucy stood up and walked over to Tanker who was still shivering from his close canine encounter. She put her arms around him and hugged him tightly.

"Tanker, my favourite lunar twin, are you all right?"

"Yeah, only I can still smell that dog's breath! It was awful. A mixture of vomit and raw meat."

"You were great! You didn't flinch."

"Yeah, Tank," Yeoman too was impressed. "You were dead cool, man!"

"Cool? I wasn't cool! I was frozen solid. I thought that dog was going to swallow me in one bite."

"There is just one thing that is bothering me though," Lucy was looking at them both. "Would one of you mind telling me what in the name of God is going on?"

Tanker began to explain.

"Mm... It's sort of my fault. But we've been sort of kid... "

" ...Kidnapped! Yes, I've sort of gathered that. Being thrown into a Hiace van, tied up, blindfolded and then locked up in a dungeon would suggest that! The question is, why? Why have I been kidnapped? I mean, I share a corporation flat with a mother who reads palms for a living. I'm not exactly big ransom material, am I?"

Tanker sat down beside her. He sighed deeply before explaining what had happened that day. He told her about sorting the photos and seeing those of Joe and the Diner. How the Biker's real name was Paul Duffy and how he called in himself to collect his pictures. He told her how he had replaced the four negatives with four blanks and filled in the "Poor Light" box on the outer envelope.

"And you thought that a hardened criminal like Duffy would say 'Oh dear. Poor light. I must make sure my flash is working in future!'" Lucy threw her eyes up to heaven and lit a cigarette. She threw one to Yeoman and offered one to Tanker. He felt like a condemmed man being offered a smoke as a last request. Why not? he thought.

Lucy held the lighter to his cigarette and he sucked but nothing happened. He tried again and suddenly a cloud of smoke rushed into his mouth which he instantly expelled.

The smoke tasted awful but at least concentrating on how to hold a cigarette without looking like a nerd gave him something to do. He took small puffs which he exhaled immediately. Then, as he thought he was growing more confident, he tried to blow out the smoke in rings, just like Denis, but this meant keeping some smoke in his mouth which in turn meant swallowing some. He coughed and spluttered and felt his head spin.

"Are you okay?" Lucy was still sitting next to him but her voice seemed much further away.

"Remind me to give these up when we get out of here!"

"Yeah, Tanker." Yeoman didn't sound too happy. "If ever!"

"We will!" Tanker nodded, trying to be reassuring, as he gave up on the smoke bubbles and sat watching the cigarette smouldering between his fingers.

"So you'll be able to get those negatives for Duffy in the morning?" Lucy asked.

"Er... no."

"What do you mean 'er... no'! You hid them in the darkroom

store, didn't you? You told me you put them in an envelope!" Yeoman was practically screaming.

"Well I did... sort of... " Even though it was dark Tanker was aware that they were both staring anxiously at him.

"I mean I did... I put them in an envelope... at first... " he was afraid to tell them what he did next.

"Then what? What the hell did you do with that envelope?"

"Well, I was going to post them to Sergeant Donnelly when I was doing Sean's post. But then I saw this guard on duty outside the GPO. I asked him did he know Sergeant Donnelly. He said he did so I asked him would he give the envelope to him."

"You what?" Yeoman couldn't believe what he had just heard. "How could you have been so stupid? The guards! You actually gave those shots to Donnelly... I don't believe this! Of all the dumb... Did you send him a love letter as well? Sod it, Tanker, you are a total moron! A dial M for Moron!"

"Now just a minute!" Lucy was now attacking Yeoman. "If anyone around here deserves to be called a moron it certainly isn't Tanker! You're the one who got us all in ths mess in the first place. You're the one who tried to make a name for yourself pushing dope! You're the one who got the Biker on our case! So just leave Tanker alone and do some apologising fast!"

"But why did he have to give those pictures and negatives to... "

"Shut up!"

There was a long silence. They sat down with their cigarettes glowing like tiny red torches in the cold darkness of the cellar. Lucy put her head on Tanker's shoulder.

"Sorry, Tanker." Yeoman's apology was barely audible but Tanker was glad he heard it.

"It's okay, Yeoman. I suppose it was a dumb thing to do. But it was either him or Sean. At least Donnelly will know the right thing to do. I did write him a note as well as it happens. I gave him the Biker's name and phone number. I told him about the pictures of the pub in Blackpool."

Yeoman had cooled down. Even though he was still annoyed with Tanker, Lucy's outburst had put him in his place.

"I suppose Donnelly might have enough to put the Biker away, but only after he's finished with us. And you can be sure the Queen will get off scot free! The Biker won't open his mouth about her."

Lucy sighed out loud. There was no point in going on like this all night. They had to be ready for the Biker in the morning. It was time to change the subject.

"If there's one thing I hate more than being kidnapped it's being kidnapped on an empty stomach! I'm starving!"

"Me too!" Tanker groaned.

"No pizza tonight, folks!" Yeoman stated the obvious as they all groaned.

Chapter 23

A Kiss Under The Goldie Fish

Yeoman snoozed fitfully on the floor, muttering every five minutes about how cold and hungry he was. Tanker and Lucy sat with their backs to the stone wall. Lucy had snuggled in close to keep warm. Tanker liked the feel of her up close to him. Every now and then Lucy would break away and light another cigarette. Tanker smoked too, even though the taste still made him feel nauseous. It was a way of passing the time.

He feared what the morning would bring. The Biker had shown him before how vicious he could be. Now with his gang and that dog he had the capacity to be even more violent. How could he have been so stupid to have believed that he could have fooled the Biker? Why hadn't he told Sean? Why did he not telephone Sergeant Donnelly immediately? Why did he not tell the guard outside the GPO what was in the envelope?

At two o'clock he heard the familiar peel of Shandon Bells. Situated on top of one of the Northside's steep hills, Shandon was a landmark. A huge golden salmon was affixed to the weather vane on its steeple, which locals called the Goldie Fish. Those living within the sound of the bells lived "Under the Goldie Fish".

He nudged Lucy to tell her that he thought they were near Shandon. They had heard the bells earlier but none of them had taken any notice. Lucy didn't move. She had fallen asleep. Tanker liked the feel of her there snuggled into his chest. He rubbed the outside of her arm gently and she snuggled even tighter.

He couldn't sleep. His mind was too alert. He felt like a trapped animal awaiting a pouncing beast. Staying awake was his defence mechanism. He thought about the changes in his life in recent months. He thought of his parents and how happy they seemed to be again. His father had definitely changed this time. This time he meant it. It wasn't just Robin Hood talk. He really seemed to have learned his lesson.

The argument between his mother and father on the morning of his father's release seemed so far away now. Remembering it wasn't so painful. Remembering it now, he felt guilty for blaming his mother. She was entitled to her anger. His father had to be more responsible. She was doing her best to cope and if he wanted to be a permanent part of their lives then he would have to start now. In hindsight, her outburst seemed as natural as it was necessary.

And what about his own outburst? Screaming at his father like that. Was that natural? Was that necessary? He didn't think so now. In fact he felt he had been a bit unfair. What good was it bringing all that hurt up? So his father was never there when he needed him as a younger child. So his father missed the big occasions like his communion and his first match for the Rovers. What was the point in dwelling on all that lonely stuff? Sure, it did hurt a lot at the time. But that was then. What was important was now. His father was back now and was doing his best to make up for lost time.

As the pre-dawn minutes ticked away in that cold cellar Tanker began to fill up with guilt. He made a promise that he would never hurt his father like that again. He promised that he would never refer to any of that stuff again. He prayed that he would get a chance to keep such promises.

The bells chimed on the quarter of the hour.

"That's Shandon, Lucy. We must still be on the northside!"

Lucy sighed on wakening. She turned her face slightly to face him.

"What did you say?"

"Those bells. Shandon Bells. I'd recognise them anywhere! We're under the Goldie Fish!" He sounded excited.

Lucy frowned. As if being near Shandon made any difference, she thought. Tanker was looking at her, waiting for a comment.

"Yes, Tanker, we're in a dungeon on the northside and we can hear Shandon Bells. Aren't we the lucky ones!"

Her voice was cynical but she wasn't angry. She gave him a full smile and kissed his cheek. Even though it was only his cheek it was different. It wasn't her usual sisterly peck. She didn't look away. She settled her head on his chest again but kept her eyes fixed on his.

"Still," she said softly, "the company isn't bad."

"Do you mean that?"

"Ssh...." she whispered, "you'll wake Yeoman."

She smiled at him again. Then without warning she put her hand to the back of his head and brought his face down to meet hers. Before he knew what was happening she was kissing him. There was definitely nothing sisterly about this. She opened her mouth on his. Tanker held her tightly. He wanted to giggle as her nose-rings were tickling his upper lip but he was afraid that she would laugh too and then they would stop. The last thing he wanted was for this to stop. He felt he was in some sort of hypnotic trance as she moved her lips ever so gently on his before slipping her head on to the side of his neck.

"I just wanted to see what it would be like," she whispered in his ear. "Just in case we... "

" ...Ssh... " This time it was Tanker who stopped her in mid-sentence. "Don't say any more!" He stroked her cheek and she kept her head there and settled back to sleep. Please God, thought Tanker, don't let the morning come.

Chapter 24

Dog's Dinner

Tanker was beginning to doze as Shandon Bells chimed again. Four o'clock. He realised, however, that it wasn't just the pre-dawn peeling that had disturbed him. During the night he had heard voices from the room above the cellar. Now the voices were louder. He could hear more laughter, the sound of bottles clinking and the occasional outburst of aggressive barking.

"Lucy, can you hear that?" he whispered to her as she lay cradled on his shoulder. "They sound as if they're drinking!"

"Yeah," Lucy raised her head sleepily. "They must be having a party. Nice of them to invite us!" She put her head down again.

"It's not funny, Lucy. What if they decide to come back down?"

"Let's hope they don't!" Yeoman was awake now too.

The three lay still listening to the sounds overhead. Suddenly they heard footsteps, but not from the room above them. They were coming from the steps outside.

Tanker froze. He was gripped with fear as the door was opened. He closed his eyes and hoped that it would all go away. That it was all a bad dream. That any moment now he would wake up and find himself at home in his own bed.

He kept his eyes tightly shut. Lucy lay huddled close to him as if she too was trying to wish it all away.

Tanker inhaled deeply. He was conscious that somebody was standing over him. He braced himself for that kick, that punch, that beating which he was sure would follow. Why else would they want to come back into the cellar at this hour?

He opened his eyes and peered over Lucy's shoulder. Staring him in the face was the rottweiler.

"We thought you might like to feed him?" The voice was

that of the van driver. He was a short well-built man, not unlike his dog. It was difficult to figure out his age as his balaclava hid most of his face. His speech was slurred as if he had had too much to drink before coming down into the cellar.

"I think we'll play 'William Tell'!" suggested his companion, who had the same rottweiler-build and face hidden by a balaclava.

Tanker was pulled to his feet and blindfolded.

"Leave him alone!" It was Lucy screaming rather than pleading.

Tanker heard the slap as Lucy was told to shut it. He was dragged across the cellar and his hands were tied behind his back. He was pushed into a hard chair to which he was bound tightly.

"Just pour it on to his head!"

Pour what? Tanker shuddered. Petrol? Were they going to set him on fire? Tar? Maybe they were going to tar and feather him? Please God no!

Suddenly his nostrils were filled with the pungent stench of dogfood. There was much drunken giggling from the two minders as the meat was rubbed into his hair as if it were shampoo. Slivers of bloody meat trickled down his cheeks and on to his lips. The taste made Tanker want to retch. Somewhere in the darkness of the cellar the dog's growling was growing more pronounced. Tanker was terrified. He wanted to scream out loud but knew this would only make matters worse. He heard a chink as the dog's leash was detached from its collar.

"Go boy! Go eat your dinner!"

Tanker was pushed back in the chair as the dog pounced on him. He could feel the hot, panting breath on his face as the dog devoured the meat. The sharp claws dug deep into Tanker's shirt, scratching the flesh beneath. Teeth grazed his scalp with every gulping bite. Tanker battled to stay calm as wave after wave of terror washed through him.

"Just keep still, Tanker! He won't bite you if you keep still!"

"Stay cool, Tank! He only wants the meat!"

He could hear Lucy and Yeoman screaming while the dog-handler and his accomplice laughed uncontrollably. Tanker tried to focus his mind on other things. He tried to block out what was happening. There is no dog, he told himself. This is not happening. Time to wake up soon. This is not happening. No dog. Not happening. No dog! No dog! No dog!

"What in the name of God are you doing? Get that bloody dog away from him!" It was the Biker who was obviously not too pleased. "I told the pair of you to stay upstairs until I got back. You were not to come back down here!"

"Sorry, boss!"

"They were making a lot of noise down here."

"We decided to teach them a lesson!"

"No harm done, boss!"

"Just a quick game of 'William Tell'!"

"Call that beast off him! Now!"

Tanker sighed out loud as the dog was pulled from him.

"Making noise, were you?" the Biker sneered at them.

"No, Mr Duffy! We were asleep!" Yeoman was grovelling again.

"Shut up, Dunne! Now, one more sound out of any of you before morning and I'll come down here to deal with you myself."

He slammed the cellar door behind him. Lucy and Yeoman ran over to Tanker and untied him.

"Jesus, Tanker! I thought you were dead." Yeoman told him as Tanker got to his feet and began furiously rubbing the remains of the dog's dinner from his hair.

"Look, let's just sit down and try not to disturb them," Lucy advised them as she handed out the last of her cigarettes.

They sat silently smoking. Above them they could hear muffled voices. While they knew that the Biker wasn't happy about the last attack, they were also aware of how vicious he could be himself. They would speak very little for the rest of the night.

"Let's all try and get some sleep," Lucy suggested long after the last of the cigarettes had been stubbed out on the cold stone floor. Yeoman got up and walked to the far side of the cellar where he lay down. Lucy put her arms around Tanker and kissed his cheek.

"Are you okay, Tommy?"

Tanker sighed deeply.

"I am now, Lu!"

She rocked him gently as the terror that had besieged him earlier gave way to a fitful sleep.

"Jesus, Tanker! Lucy! They've gone mad! Listen to that! They're wrecking the place upstairs." Yeoman was standing over Tanker and Lucy. In the room above them it sounded as if furniture was being thrown against walls. There was scuffling and angry shouting.

"What are they doing?" Lucy sprang to her feet scratching her head.

"They must have flipped this time!" Yeoman was screaming. "That's glass breaking! They'll take it out on us! I know it! They're going to kill us! I just know it!"

"Oh damn it!" Tanker gulped. "They're coming down the steps!"

Suddenly there was a pounding on the door of the cellar.

"Why don't they just open it? They've got keys!"

When the door burst open all they could see were the beams of torches seeking them out in the dark.

"Everbody down!" came the order and the three of them immediately obeyed, throwing themselves to the cold concrete floor of the cellar. Tanker once more braced himself for the worst.

In seconds they were pinned to the ground. When the torch was shone into his face Tanker's terror gave way to instant joy. He could hear Yeoman whooping with delight.

"It's the cops! The cops! Thanks be to Christ for that!"

Chapter 25

Making Statements

Once the guards had ascertained that none of them were members of the Biker's gang they were brought by squad car to the garda station to give their statements. All their parents were there in the waiting room. There was a prolonged hugging and kissing and crying session with "Thank God you're all right!" "I was out of mind with worry!" "I thought you were all dead!" being said over and over again, before each of the three was asked to go and give a statement.

Tanker was taken to a washroom where he had a shower before going to make his statement. He stood soaping himself under the warm water spray for ages. It felt good to scrub the caked-in dogfood from his hair and the apple scent of shampoo helped him forget the smell of the rottweiler's breath.

In Interview Room One, Tanker gave his account of the events of the previous day to Sergeant Donnelly who kept telling him that, although he did the right thing in sending him the snaps, he should have phoned him immediately.

"I don't think you realised how much danger you were in. When I got those pictures I was worried about your safety. I called immediately to your flat but there was no reply. Then when Mrs Higgins reported her daughter Lucy missing I went back to check Eamon Dunne's flat only to discover that his parents thought he was with you. We thought you might have all gone to Denis Cummins' house but he told us he hadn't seen you all day. He also told us of the other incidents involving you and Duffy. You should have come to us about those, Tom."

Tanker couldn't have agreed more.

"But how did you know where we were?"

"It was quite routine, really. We had been watching Duffy for some time. We went looking for him last night. We searched his house. We searched other houses we knew he either owned or regularly frequented and eventually we found you in the basement of that disused pub which he had just bought."

"So will you be charging him with Joe's murder?"

"I can't answer that, Tom. As you might appreciate, that would be confidential. Let's just say we hope Mr Duffy gets what's coming to him."

"And the Queen? You know, Mary Glynn. Everybody knows she's the big boss."

Donnelly sighed. He scratched his greying head with his pen before resting it on his hand.

"Sorry, Tom. No comment. I can't discuss that one. I'm sorry."

Tanker was dismayed. After all they had been through the previous day there still might not be enough evidence to put the Queen away.

Donnelly was anxious to change the subject.

"Come on, you must be starving. I'll organise some breakfast for you and your friends. How does a large fry sound to you?"

Despite his disappointment Tanker's stomach seemed to speak for him. It rumbled almost in reflex response to the offer of breakfast.

"Like an angel dancing on my intestines!"

Tanker ate breakfast with his parents. His father joked about how he had never been offered a fry in a garda station before.

"Any time I gave a statement the most I ever got was a cold cup of tea and a ciggie. Plenty of porridge though!" He laughed at his own joke. His wife glared at him.

"Keep your voice down, Tom! Anyway, I thought I told you, no more prison jokes!"

"Sorry, love, it's just that it's kind of funny being here on a voluntary basis. Look at this, for God's sake." He pointed to the guest identity badge he had pinned on his jacket. "The last time I was here the only thing they pinned on me was a house break-in! That and a pair of handcuffs!"

The three of them laughed then. Tanker enjoyed the laughter. It was good sitting there listening to his father's jokes and watching his mother's reactions. He hoped it would last.

On the way home to the flat Tanker told them both the whole story from start to finish leaving out no detail. Ann Kelly smiled when she thought of the letter she wrote to the corporation about the slippery steps.

"Still, at least some good came out of it. Benny is constantly mopping and drying them now. They haven't looked as clean in years."

Tom Senior kept saying how he knew all along that Tanker was hiding something.

"I knew something was up the night of the fire when you walked out after shouting at me. You were upset. I knew you had something on your mind!"

"Sorry about that, Dad. I shouldn't have... "

"Stop!" His father wouldn't let him continue. "That's all water under the bridge now. Forget about it."

Yeah, thought Tanker, it's all water under the bridge, let's forget it.

When they got home Tanker was exhausted. He went straight to bed. His mind was racing with jumbled thoughts, some good, some bad. Lucy's kiss, his parents being together, the Biker's finger on his chin, the smell of the rottweiler's breath, the smell of the cellar, his dad's job, the darkness, his dad's jokes, a Hiace van, his mother's letter, the envelope with the snaps and negatives, Joe, Benny mopping the steps, the fire, the smell of dogfood, the identity badge on his dad's jacket, Lucy's kiss again, Joe again, Lucy's nose-ring tickling, Yeoman hugging his dad in the waiting-room, smoking cigarettes, Shandon Bells... ding dong, ding dong... ding dong, ding dong...

Chapter 26

No Case To Answer

The following Saturday Tanker was working once again. Sean had called to the flat on the Tuesday while Tanker was sleeping off the effects of his ordeal the previous night. He told Ann that he wanted Tanker and Yeoman to work alternate weekends. Tanker was delighted. He was relieved that Sean didn't seem to mind that he hadn't consulted him about the photographs.

He had just finished delivering a parcel of cards for Sean and was putting the bike in the storeroom when he heard Sean on the phone. He sounded disappointed.

"So that's it then?... No luck?... Yeah I know... It was never going to be easy... You did your best... At least you got something to pin on that rat Duffy... Yeah, I hope he does too... Two years?... Is that all?... Okay thanks... I appreciate your phoning me... Yeah, of course... strictly off the record... Okay, bye."

He slammed the receiver down and cursed out loud. Tanker put his head around the door and waited for Sean to speak. He didn't. He just threw his eyes towards the ceiling and sighed deeply.

"Bad news?"

"You could say that, Tanker. That was a friend of mine. I went to school with him. He's a detective in the drug squad. The Queen was released today without charge. She's got away with it."

"Damn!" Tanker was disgusted

"They've nothing on her, Tanker. Duffy is afraid to spill the beans. He's facing a few years for assault and kidnapping, maybe more for possession with intent to supply. They found nothing in that pub or in his house to link him with the fire. They found plenty of drugs though. All sorts of stuff hidden in empty beer kegs. Apparently they even found some in the toilet cisterns and more in the pockets of shirts he had hanging on his clothesline at home."

"But what about Joe?"

"As I said, they found nothing to link him to either the fire or Joe's death. That's what my friend phoned me for!"

Tanker couldn't believe it. Not enough evidence? Duffy had kidnapped them to get Joe's photograph back. What more evidence did the guards need?

Sean couldn't have agreed more. However, his friend told him that Duffy was being very clever. He was denying kidnapping. He was claiming that all he wanted to do was to give Yeoman a fright. That he had gone back during the night to let them go but that the police had arrested him before he got the chance. He admitted to being a small-time drugs dealer, and said that Yeoman had owed him money. As for the pictures of Joe, he simply said that photography was his hobby. He liked to take pictures of buildings. Joe's Diner was one of the best known landmarks in the city. There was no law against taking pictures.

Later that night Tanker, Yeoman and Lucy stood on the balcony of the fourth floor and looked down on the car-park. Tanker had told them the bad news. They each felt helpless.

"Like there's nothing we can do. If the guards can't find a case for them to answer, what can we do?" Tanker looked at Lucy as he spoke. He waited for her to pipe up with something chirpy and optimistic.

"You did your best, Tanker. We all did. Maybe in the next life we'll all come back as superheroes and rid the world of drugs, crime and corruption!"

Yeoman frowned at her.

"Yeah, Lucy! And maybe in this life Duffy is going to come back here as a madman and rid the world of me!"

They went into Tanker's flat to watch *Match of the Day*.

They had come out onto the balcony because they didn't want to be tempted to look up the score on Teletext before the programme began. Tanker made the tea and threw a packet of fig-rolls on the coffee table. The three of them settled down in front of the telly.

"Who's playing?" Lucy didn't know a lot about soccer.

"Arsenal and Newcastle."

"Which is which?"

"Newcastle are the black and whites, Arsenal are red." Tanker was being patient.

"Who's the fat guy playing for?"

"What fat guy?"

"The fellow in the greeny black."

"He's the referee, you plonker!" Yeoman wasn't being as patient as Tanker.

"Come on, Newcastle!" Lucy was pretending to take an interest.

"Why are you going for Newcastle?" Yeoman asked her.

"Better bums! Look at his there, that number five! Wow! Good ass, man! Good behind! A ten for number five!"

"Lucy, good bums have got nothing to do with how good a team is! Now be quiet and let us watch it!"

"Well you've a good bum and you're a good player!"

"Ssh... " Tanker blushed as he tried to quieten her.

"Anyway, there's another reason why I'm going to shout for Newcastle!"

"Why?" Tanker asked.

"They won four-three... penalty in the last minute. I heard it on the early evening news!"

Yeoman was just about to fire a cushion at her when Tom and Ann Kelly came back from the pub.

"Hi, you lot!" Tom Kelly Senior waved on his way to the kitchen. "What are you watching?"

Match of the Day!" Tanker mumbled.

"Newcastle and Arsenal," Yeoman added.

"Oh yeah, I heard about that on the news. Four-three to Newcastle... penalty in the last minute!"

"Thanks, Dad!"

They watched the rest of the game without interruption. When it was over Lucy and Yeoman got up to go.

"Are you off home, lads?"

"Yeah goodnight Mr Kelly. Bad news today. wasn't it?"

"I suppose so," he said calmly.

"Suppose so?" Yeoman sounded confused. "They got away with it, Mr Kelly. The Biker will get a few years and the Queen won't even be charged. She has no case to answer."

"No case to answer? To answer to who?"

Yeoman shook his head. Tanker wasn't sure either. What was his father on about? Had he had too much to drink?

"To the guards, Dad! To the courts!"

Tom Kelly Senior grinned.

"To us. Maybe she might have a case to answer to us!"

Chapter 27

Operation De-Throne

Sean loved the idea.

"Tanker, you're a genius!"

"It's not my idea. It's me dad's!"

"Then he's a genius! And you're a son of a genius!"

"Well, if you put it like that... "

"But we're going to have to work very hard to pull it off. It's going to take a lot of work. But I reckon it will be worth it! What do you think, Yeoman?"

"I'm in!"

They arranged a meeting in the studio for that very night. Tanker and his parents were there as were Yeoman and his. Celia was working but she said she'd be able to help on the big night. Lucy and her mother came. Denis arrived with his father. Tom Kelly and Eddie Dunne had brought along several of the neighbours from Terence MacSwiney Mansions. All seemed eager to do something about the Queen.

Sean spoke briefly, outlining the plan. It was simple. He would organise the posters. He would have them ready by Saturday. With Denis' help he would take the photographs of her himself using his zoom lens. He would make out some fliers as well which they could put through letterboxes. Tom Kelly said he would organise the ladders from work. Denis's father agreed to provide some of his taxi-fleet for transport.

So that was that. Operation De-Throne. Sunday morning next. Two am.

Chapter 28

Leaving On A Jet Plane

Tanker couldn't wait to hear the early Sunday morning news. He sat with Lucy, Denis and Yeoman in the kitchen. His mother had prepared a huge fry which they had devoured. Being up all night had left them famished. They whooped with delight when they heard the first item on the national nine o'clock news.

"Residents in Cork City are waking this morning to see their city littered with blunt messages for a certain Ms Mary Glynn. Banners have been hung from every bridge over the River Lee. Walls and telegraph poles are bedecked with posters, each with the same blunt message. "Mary Glynn, Drug Baron, Out." Our Southern Correspondent Tom Gleeson believes this to be the work of a newly-formed group "Concerned Northsiders Against Drugs". The posters and banners are believed to refer to a Ms Mary Glynn who has been the centre of recent gardaí enquiries into drug trafficking and extortion rackets in the Cork area... "

It had been the greatest night in Tanker's life. He thought originally that there would be no more than a dozen or so of them involved. However, as word of the new group spreads more and more residents from the Mansions and the neighbouring flat complexes volunteered to get involved. On the night itself over two hundred volunteers plastered the area with banners, posters and fliers. It was like an all-night carnival as Operation De-Throne sprang to life. The normally silent, almost threatening, streets buzzed with activity. The message was delivered loud and clear. Mary Glynn. Drug Baron. Out.

Tanker had gone with his father and Lucy. They were in charge of door-to-door fliers in all the flats. Yeoman, Eddie and Denis had been on similar duty in the more affluent Cnoc Barra area where Mary Glynn had her "palace". By early morning the whole area looked like it was in the middle of a General Election campaign. Mary Glynn's face was everywhere. Her name was splashed over every newspaper headline. Tanker had orgainsed that. He took great delight contacting the press before dawn on Sean's mobile phone.

"Hello is that RTÉ? This is Tom Kelly of the Concerned Northsiders Against Drugs. It might be a good idea to send a camera crew to the Blackpool area... Sure this is genuine!... Yes, you can phone me back to verify... "

Yeoman and Denis went home after breakfast. Tanker was tired but he was too excited to sleep. He sat on the couch with Lucy. Since the night in the cellar neither of them had mentioned "the kiss". Tanker felt uneasy about it. It wasn't that he hadn't enjoyed it. Far from it. He had really enjoyed it. Thinking about it and reliving it in his mind had been a constant source of pleasure for him ever since. But he wasn't sure as to what would happen next. Would they do it again? Would snogging become a regular part of their relationship from now on? One voice inside his head was saying "yes please!" Another voice was saying "not so sure that would be such a good idea!" As he sat next to her on the couch the "not so sure" voice was winning even though the "yes please" voice was doing its best to be heard. In the end he didn't have to make a choice.

"Tanker... " she stopped to give him to time to say "Yes, Lucy?" He obliged.

"Yes, Lucy?"

"No more snogging! Okay?"

"Fine, Lucy."

"I kissed you in the cellar because I was afraid. That was all."

"I understand. No sweat." He lied.

"I was afraid and you were looking after me. It felt nice being held by you."

"It was nice for me, too." Tanker was eager to add. Just in case she wasn't sure.

"You were being so brave about everything, I just got the urge to kiss you. Properly."

"And?" Tanker was anxious to know more.

"And nothing."

"Nothing?"

"No, Tanker. That was it. I kissed you. You kissed me. That was all."

"Did you like it?"

"It was okay."

"Only okay!" Tanker was disappointed. Only okay! His head had nearly blown off his shoulders and all she could say was "only okay".

"Well, it was lovely and all that. But it was a bit like kissing my own brother!"

"Oh really! You don't have your own brother!"

"You know what I mean. Anyway. That's where you come in. I look on you as a brother."

Tanker felt deflated again. He felt a sudden urge to get on his REM tape and play *Everybody Hurts*. However, as he looked at Lucy twiddling her plait he knew she was right. He thought she must have had a "yes please"voice and a "not so sure that would be such a good idea" voice too. Only her "not so sure" voice was obviously much louder than his.

"So that's it, Tanker. I hope you don't mind but that's how I feel. It would be crazy going out with each other. We're too close. Maybe in the next life!"

"Maybe!" He smiled at her. Time for a quick change of subject. "Your head could do with a shave, Lucy. It's getting all patchy."

She smiled back.

"You could do with a shave yourself. Your upper lip is getting really hairy."

Tanker grinned. She had noticed! At last somebody had

noticed. He was just about to ask her had she noticed how his spots had cleared up when there was a banging on the door. It was Sean.

"I won't come in, Tanker. Just pass on the good news to everybody. I just got a call from RTÉ news. The Queen flew out of Cork Airport this morning. She's fled the country. She's gone!"

Chapter 29

No More Kick The Can

Tanker woke up early on the following Saturday morning. He had no work and had planned to stay in bed all day. Outside he heard the familiar grating of tin can on tarmac. Dunnzer was once again taking charge. Tanker got up and looked out. He was going to shout down at them but didn't bother. He lay down on his bed and dozed.

The events of the previous weekend still danced around in his mind. The Queen was gone and that made him feel happy. He had seen her on the news the day she flew out of the country. She brushed past reporters refusing to answer any questions, shielding her face from clicking cameras and microphones. She wasn't at all as he had imagined her. She looked like anybody's granny. Two-piece suit, blue rinsed perm, big glasses. As she hastened towards the departure lounge with her head bowed Tanker stood up and shook his fist at the screen.

"Good riddance!"

At school that week he met Denis in the canteen. Denis told him that, much to the delight of the local residents in Cnoc Barra, Glynn's house was up for sale. She obviously felt safer in exile. At least they had achieved that. Joe's death had been in some way avenged. But it wasn't all good news.

Tanker was disappointed that nothing had really changed. He knew it wouldn't be long before some other dealer would move in and claim the flats as his or her territory. Only the previous night, as himself and Yeoman headed out for yet another school disco, a couple of strangers asked them did they know of anybody selling. The disco had been a diappointment too. Yeoman spent the night trying to impress Helen O'Sullivan again, while Tanker spent the night watching him fail again.

In the kitchen he heard his father making breakfast. He had come off his nightshift and was going to spend the rest of the day in bed. Tanker went in to the kitchen to join him.

They sat sipping tea, munching toast and recalling the events of the previous weekend.

"I dunno, Dad. Was it all worth it?"

"What do you mean? Of course it was! Glynn is gone!"

"Yeah, I know but it won't be long before someone else muscles in. Dealers don't just disappear. "

"Then we'll push them out, son. We'll keep our own patch clean. I was talking to Eddie Dunne about it. We're thinking of getting the Residents Association up and running again. He's dead keen. We can form a full-time Concerned Residents Against Drugs. We can keep this thing going, Tanker, don't you worry."

"Ah but for how long, Dad?"

"For as long as it takes, son!" He stopped eating and put his hands up to his ears.

"Who the hell is kicking that bloody can down there?"

"It's just Dunnzer and the other kids playing the FA Cup Final. They do it every weekend. Stay where you are. I'll throw them down the ball... "

"Ball!" Tom Kelly Senior jumped to his feet. "I nearly forgot!" He went over to the cupboard and pulled out a round parcel. "This came for you yesterday while you were at school. I went off to bed and forgot all about it."

Tanker tore off the paper. There it was. One Regulation Weight, Limited Edition, Premier League, in Conjunction with Coca-Cola, Superball. He had got it with the ring-pulls Joe had saved for him. He held the ball in his lap then bounced it gently on his knee. He saw Joe's face on the ball with every bounce.

"Nice ball, isn't it, son?"

"Yeah, Dad. It's great."

"Who sent it to you?"

"It's sort of a present."

"From who?"

"Ah, it doesn't matter, Dad. Look you go to bed. I'll tidy up here."

"But I told your mother I'd bring her up some breakfast... "

"I'll do that!"

"Are you sure?"

"Yeah."

"Okay, son. I'm bushed. Good night, I mean, good morning! I'll never get used to this nightwork!"

Tanker got up and walked over to the window.

"Hey, Dunnzer!" he shouted.

"Hi, Tank! Can we borrow your ball?"

"Here! You can have this one! For keeps! But for God's sake, will you stop kicking that bloody can! There are people up here trying to get some sleep!"

ANOTHER GREAT BOOK FROM

BLACKWATER PRESS

Kirsten Donnelly's family leave Northern Ireland for a life of peace in the Scottish Highlands and to escape the violence that tragically took the life of her father.

But for Kirsten the move is much more than a simple change of address. Her new home is far from the bustle of Belfast and her life-long friends...

Suddenly, she feels very lost and alone.

Life starts to look good again when she meets with Douglas MacLennan and his gang, but, her new popularity has its price...

Will she be tempted by the ecstasy of drugs? Will she steal for it, will she get caught? Is she prepared to risk her future for these new friends?

Just how far will Kirsten go in order to be accepted?

£3.99